S.M. LEVINE

Over Work

First published by S.M. Levine 2025

This novel is entirely a work of fiction. The names, characters and incidents portrayed in it are the work of the author's imagination. Any resemblance to actual persons, living or dead, events or localities is entirely coincidental.

The author does not consent to any Artificial Intelligence (AI), generative AI, large language model, machine learning, chatbot, or other automated analysis, generative process, or replication program to reproduce, mimic, remix, summarize, or otherwise replicate any part of this creative work, via any means: print, graphic, sculpture, multimedia, audio, or other medium. The author supports the right of humans to control their artistic works. No part of this book has been created using AI-generated images or narrative, as known by the author.

First edition

ISBN: 979-8-9919826-6-5

This book was professionally typeset on Reedsy.
Find out more at reedsy.com

For my family

Contents

Preface

Dear Reader,

Thank you so much for choosing my book! Cameron and Sasha's story is the third and final book in The Well Space series, and while it can be read as a standalone, the books work best when read in order.

Cameron exists in a state of constant burnout. Work has become almost an addiction for him. When he meets Sasha, he learns not only how to relax and have fun again, but also how to find meaning and joy through his work.

It would be oversimplifying to say that Sasha has an anger management problem. She has an injustice problem, because the world has treated her unfairly too many times. But she discovers that having one person on your side—the right person—makes all the difference.

Over Work is an open-door contemporary romance. Tropes include: opposites attract, nerd (him)/jock (her), and friends to lovers. Trigger warnings for the book include: depictions of burnout and anxiety, discussions of addiction, vandalism (off page), physical violence (off page), incidents of hate crimes (off page), discussions of probation and imprisonment. If this content might be triggering for you, please take care and consider if reading this book is right for you.

I loved writing this story! It made me a little sad to type "the end" on the final book in this series, but I'm so excited for all the books to come next.

Happy reading,

S.M. Levine

Introduction

Letting go has never been so fun ... or so dangerous.

The last thing Sasha needs is court-mandated anger management therapy, but it's either that or spend thirty days in jail. When vandals trashed her family's food truck, her first reaction was to fight, and now she's paying the price. But when she shows up for her first counseling session, the nerdy administrative assistant there is anything but professional.

Cameron is pretty sure you can't die from overwork, but he might be close. He's struggling to function through burnout, and if he can't pull himself together, he won't graduate on time, much less get his dream job at The Well Space. To make things worse, he falls asleep in the office and wakes up to find a tattooed, dark-haired woman standing over him.

Sasha agrees not to tell Cameron's boss about his poor job performance...as long as he does her one little favor. Roped into working at Sasha's food truck over spring break, Cameron finds attraction blazing to life between them.

The more Sasha shows Cameron how to have fun, the less he feels like doing the sensible thing. But when Sasha puts herself in danger again, Cameron will have to take the leap and trust his feelings over logic.

Chapter 1

Cameron's research had shown him that everyone had a breaking point. Some breakdowns were caused by huge events, others by a tiny trigger. In many cases, the breaking point seemed tailor-made to the individual. Some people carried huge workloads with grace and stamina, but the stress left hairline cracks in them, until one additional ounce of tension brought them down.

It shouldn't have been a surprise that his own breaking point was something small and unobtrusive. A two-line email that appeared in his inbox at 8:00 p.m. on a Tuesday night.

He'd worked late again, his long frame folded under the admin assistant's desk in the third-floor waiting area of The Well Space clinic, outside of his boss Ben's office.

Ben wouldn't like it if he found out Cameron was here. This week was supposed to be his paid vacation time, time off he'd been forced to take by a boss who was way too invested in his employees' mental health and wellness. Luckily, Ben was on vacation and would never know he'd been here all week, instead of at home.

Finishing a doctoral dissertation and wrapping up a study were incompatible with taking a vacation. Some day, he would, but that day was not today. That day had not been any day in the last seven years. Today was even a special day, in theory. His birthday. But it didn't matter. Work came first, always.

The words on the laptop screen swam in front of his eyes, and he removed his wire-rimmed glasses to pinch the bridge of his nose.

Pull it together.

His normally organized, methodical brain couldn't make sense of the words in front of him. How long since his last meal? Six hours? He slid a glance over at his still-full water bottle. Hydration had also been left by the wayside this afternoon.

With extra caffeine, he could push himself to work any number of extra hours. It wasn't a matter of when, but how many every week. But lately he'd been slipping.

He squinted at the lines of text in his email inbox, his eyes shutting for a moment before blinking back into focus.

The sender, his PhD supervisor, needed his attention. His fingers moved in slow motion as he clicked the line to open the message. He shook his head, trying to clear his fuzzy vision long enough to read the message.

From: Dr. Zachary Gold
 To: Cameron Jacobs
 Subject: Data filtering

Cameron:

It appears some of the study data was filtered incorrectly.

Reports will have to be redone. Let's talk more Thursday.

Gold

Cameron blinked, his brain refusing to compute the meaning. Their year-long study on the effects of working overtime on participants' cortisol levels had ended months ago. He was in the final stretch of completing the massive data analysis. To start over on that—to start over at all—would be very bad.

If every report he'd created in the last three months had used badly filtered data, he'd be starting over from scratch.

His supervisor had included no "sorry about the sudden change" or "we'll figure this out" reassurances. That would be much too kind. Too much like a human being. He'd learned the hard way not to expect that kind of support from Dr. Gold.

There was a not-small likelihood the error had been Gold's fault, anyway. The man didn't even know the location of half the study documents. He'd said from the start that the brunt of the work for this study would fall on Cameron's shoulders if he expected a doctorate to come out of it. If not for Cameron's hard work, Gold wouldn't have a study to publish at all.

But this was his degree on the line. His future. One day, he'd finish this program and never have to lay eyes on Dr. Zachary Gold again.

He dragged his gaze away from the laptop screen and scanned the room, as if the darkened office held some answer. The Well Space was quiet after hours. The clinic—located in a stately old Victorian home—radiated comfort, from the antique furnishings to the soft floral rugs. The therapists' offices were all refurbished bedrooms, and the living areas had been transformed into comfy sitting lounges.

All he'd ever wanted was to be a therapist on staff here. There was no other goal, not since he'd first walked in the door for his interview three years ago.

Even if he did feel disconnected from his goal these days. A dull filter covered everything in his brain, like a dirty windshield.

Weeks of work had just been tossed out the window. He'd never minded hard work, but this was wasted work, something much worse.

He reached for the trackpad to transfer the email attachment into the correct folder. He stopped in mid-air, his brain searching for the folder's location on his laptop. He never misplaced files, but for the life of him, he couldn't navigate his own hard drive right now. His hand shook on the mouse.

He should eat something. His last meal had been breakfast, a bagel grabbed before he left the apartment.

He stood on unsteady legs and scrubbed his hands over his face. The kitchen downstairs had crackers. Maybe even a frozen dinner someone had abandoned. Walking away from the laptop and down the steps felt like the right choice, even if it meant more wasted time.

It did no good to get angry or frustrated. Grad school had taught him that. Hell, life had taught him from early on. People who let their emotions rule them had more messes to clean up.

So he wasn't upset as he left his desk and went downstairs in search of food. But his brain felt off, slow and laggy. His mind should have been racing ahead right now, trying to figure out how he would fix this mess. Instead, it was a car with the check-engine light on. Not even a spark of an idea of how to work with this.

A sliver of unease went up his spine. His ability to focus had always been the one thing he had that other people didn't. If his brain didn't work anymore, he wasn't worth much.

In the clinic's kitchen, he munched on some dry saltines and a piece of string cheese, and even remembered to down a glass of tap water. Then, instead of heading back upstairs to get back to work, his feet took him down the hall to the first-floor corner office occupied by Matt, one of the newer therapists on staff.

He stood in the doorway of Matt's office, where the comfy armchairs sat at angles to one another in the corner. Matt had a polished oak desk and a tall window with a view of the dark night sky.

He'd always wanted an office with a window.

He entered the room and sank into Matt's desk chair. It was plush and deep, with soft upholstery.

Matt had gone home on time, like most employees of The Well Space did. Since Ben had made work hours stricter and PTO mandatory, everyone followed the rules. Everyone except Cameron.

But he wasn't a full staff member yet. Just an assistant. His head lolled back against the chair's high back.

Just an assistant. So far.

In his dreams, he pictured Ben offering him a job here after graduation, as a licensed therapist. Ben was currently enjoying his honeymoon and would probably have words with Cameron if he saw him here right now.

He'd promised Vanessa, Ben's partner, he'd take off the week of spring break for real. But in all likelihood, he'd be working from home on spring break, too. All the extra hours he'd put in this month meant nothing.

Nothing was a funny word. A small one, with a huge weight to it.

His eyes unfocused, gazing out at the soft light from the hallway. The office was semi-dark, quiet.

The hallway lights blurred in front of his tired eyes, and he closed them, just for a minute.

The click of footsteps made his eyes drift open. He'd fallen asleep—something he'd never done at work and had a hard time doing at home on the best days.

Or maybe he was still asleep and dreaming, because a woman stood in front of him.

His overtired brain had conjured up a tiny punk goddess, with sleek, dark hair cut to her chin, nose and eyebrow piercings, and a few visible tattoos on her chest. She wore a black leather jacket and black ripped jeans that showed off her hourglass curves.

Those were the sort of curves he'd prefer if he ever made time to haul himself onto a dating app.

Then the dream woman spoke and snapped him fully awake.

"I have a therapy session tonight. You must be Matt?" Her eyebrow rose along with the tone at the end of her sentence. She seemed unimpressed by the state of him.

He was unimpressed with himself. He sat up in a rush, brushing a hand down his rumpled dress shirt. The woman was not a product of his imagination, and in about ten seconds, the full embarrassment would hit.

"I'm sorry." He cleared his throat. "Did you say you had an appointment?"

Some of the therapists made special arrangements to meet with clients at later hours, and in those cases, they would leave the door unlocked and meet the client there. But as Ben's assistant, Cameron owned the master schedule for the entire clinic, and no one had any appointments booked for tonight.

She gave him a skeptical look. "Yes, I have an appointment for 8:00. I'm Sasha. "

"Of course." He jumped up from the couch and stretched out a hand to shake hers.

She shook it once, her grip warm and strong. Up close, he could see a tiny mole on her upper lip, how smooth her pale skin was, and the fact that her eyes were two different colors. One brown and one brown-swirled-with-blue, like a marble.

Heterochromia, his brain supplied.

He forced himself to release her hand, which he'd probably shaken a beat too long.

"So you're my new counselor," she said, dropping her hand to the side. "Guess we'll get this over with, then. You must be pretty tired, huh?"

She dropped into the chair across from his desk and looked up at him, expectant.

He blinked, trying to clear his head and let his slow brain figure out what to do next.

Matt was an amazing counselor. He was also unreliable about using the scheduling app. He'd schedule appointments and not hit save, or mark himself free when he was busy, and end up double-booked with two clients at once. This wasn't the first time Matt had managed to misplace a patient.

"Well," Cameron said helpfully.

She planted her elbows on the chair arms and leaned forward. "Aren't you going to ask me questions? Give me paperwork? Also, do you always do your sessions in the dark? Can we turn on the lights?"

"Of course." Cameron leapt from the chair and rushed to

flip the light switch. On the way, he realized one important point he needed to clarify.

"I'm not your counselor," he told her.

Her brows went down. "This is the right office, though, isn't it? He told me to meet him here, third door on the left. And the front door was unlocked, like he said it would be."

"About that… I think he must have made a mistake with his schedule. Did you get a confirmation email?"

She shook her head.

"I thought so." He sucked in a breath. "Let me text him for you. Maybe he's on his way here now."

There was no way in hell Matt was on his way here, but Cameron pulled out his cell and texted her counselor while Sasha watched him. Under her steady gaze, his fingers fumbled typing the words on the screen.

A minute later, Matt replied:

Matt: Oh my God. I am so sorry. I completely forgot to put that on the books.

Cameron: I figured.

Matt: Can you give her the intake paperwork and reschedule her appointment? At least we can have that entered for next time.

Cameron: No problem.

Matt: And what the hell are you doing still there?

Cameron: It's a long story.

He clicked his phone off and slid it into his pocket. Sasha had risen from her chair and folded her arms over her chest.

"Let me guess. He forgot." Her tone had taken on a hard edge.

"He did. He's a good guy, I promise. It was an error with his calendar."

"Typical." She shut her eyes for a minute. When they flipped open, they landed on him with laser intensity. "Do you have any idea how hard it is for me to rearrange my schedule to include these sessions? If I didn't have to…"

She broke off, drawing in a quick breath. "Never mind. I'll call him tomorrow and reschedule it. Have a good evening."

She made a move to go past him, out the door.

"Wait. Matt asked me to give you your patient intake forms. That will save you time when you come back. I can make a new appointment for you, too, so you don't have to call."

"So you do work here." She scanned him over, her eyebrow raised, and yeah, he was wrinkled from head to toe and probably sporting the heaviest five o'clock shadow known to man.

He cleared his throat again. "Yeah. I work here. I'm an administrative assistant."

"And you have a name? Not Matt, I'm assuming?"

"Cameron."

"Nice to meet you, Cameron."

"I promise I don't usually sleep at work," he told her.

The corner of her mouth tilted up. "Well, they do have you working kind of late."

She had no idea.

"They're not making me. They're really good to work for. I had some projects to take care of, and I ended up staying longer than I thought I'd need to. If you want to come upstairs, that's where my computer is."

Cameron never babbled, but he was on the verge of it, so he made himself shut his mouth.

Sasha glanced around her, as if marking the nearest exit, and he wanted to slap a palm to his forehead. She'd walked into a building alone at night, and a man she'd just met had asked her to come upstairs with him.

He needed to talk to Matt about scheduling his meetings for earlier in the day. But Matt took on patients with unusual schedules more often than the other staff members. He worked with the local court system, and a lot of his patients had been ordered into therapy by the judges.

His brain clicked on. The late hour. Her comment about getting this over with, about having to be here. He'd bet Sasha had a different background from their typical patients. If she was on parole or doing court-mandated therapy, he'd need to take special care to make her experience here a positive one.

So he needed to pull himself together because he'd already given her the worst first impression of all time.

"I really do work here," he assured her.

She smiled for the first time, a dimple appearing in her cheek. "I believe you. But only because of the suspenders." She gestured to his torso. "I don't think the bad guys wear those, and then sneak into offices and fall asleep."

People tended to notice the suspenders first. He'd worn plaid ones today, but he had an entire collection at home. Maybe they'd just helped him save face.

"I hope they don't," he told her. "Otherwise, I need to find a new way to hold up my pants."

Her smile broadened, and his breath stopped, his attention

snagging on the light reflecting off the tiny silver hoop in her nose. There was a toughness about her that made him think didn't give those smiles away easily.

Her expression shifted back into guarded territory when he didn't move from his spot.

"So…upstairs?" she prompted.

"Right." He shook his head to clear it. "This way."

Chapter 2

So far, therapy wasn't going at all how Sasha expected. The clinic space was nice, much nicer than she'd pictured a mental health clinic being. But other than that, she was less than impressed. She'd rearranged her schedule to be here for this, only to arrive and find half the lights off and her therapist asleep at his desk.

Not her therapist. An admin assistant, napping at someone else's desk. Something was wrong with this man, too. Not in an alarm-bells, creepy way, but in a 'he looked ready to fall over' kind of way.

He walked as if on a delay, his limbs uncoordinated. She'd have thought he was drunk, but his speech sounded clear and he didn't smell like booze.

Warm hazel eyes had blinked at her from behind wire-rimmed glasses as he'd come awake. For a minute, he looked lost, as if he didn't know where he was or how he'd gotten there.

He was tall and lean, with close-cut dark curls, a sharp jaw, and thick dark brows. His clothing came from another century, the wrinkled brown wool trousers, white dress shirt, and plaid suspenders making him look like an archeology professor from an old movie.

He'd surprised her into a smile by making a joke about his own attire. But this wasn't the time to let down her guard. The best outcome she could hope for was to get in, do her time here, and get out.

She should be grateful the clinic could fit her in at all. They obviously worked long hours, and dealing with patients like her—people who'd been ordered to be here against their will— couldn't be all fun and games.

She'd take the opportunity to reschedule, do her intake forms, and try not to snap at the man whose fault it wasn't.

But it was just so typical of how the system worked. In every stage of her life, from school to now, she'd been processed through the uncaring machinery of rules. The employees of places like this were always overburdened with work. The system didn't care about the individuals moving through it.

And for damn sure, no one cared about the truth or the other side of the story in cases like hers.

She squared her shoulders and followed him up the staircase. He went first, which was considerate of him. She wouldn't have appreciated him blocking her path to the exit.

Upstairs, in the third-floor waiting area, he crossed to his desk, opened his laptop, and started typing.

She sat in the cushioned armchair across from his desk, spine straight. A quick glance around the room revealed old-fashioned furniture, polished wood floors, and soft cushions. The place felt homey, which it shouldn't, considering what it was.

She was lucky this was where she'd been ordered to come. It could have been so much worse. She shuddered, thinking of a cold mental hospital or state-run clinic.

Too bad this still didn't feel like luck. More like a punishment for something that wasn't her fault. But she'd do this because the alternative was thirty days in jail, and being unable to help Dad. He needed her help, so she'd come back here for all eight mandated therapy sessions. She didn't have to like it, though.

Cameron cleared his throat. "So, the intake forms. Those will give Matt the info he needs to get started with you next time. Then we'll reschedule your appointment."

"Sounds good." She tried to keep her voice pleasant and neutral, and not remind him of the fact that she'd rearranged her whole day to be here, and the rescheduling was their fault, not hers.

"The paperwork is all on this tablet—" He broke off as he attempted to hand the device to her, fumbled it, and let it crash onto the desk.

"Sorry." He picked it up and handed it to her a second time. "The stylus is there on the side of the case."

She picked up the tablet and frowned over at him. "This paperwork is all digital. Couldn't they have sent it to me to fill out beforehand?"

"We do that, usually. But not Matt's—" He cut himself off again. "Matt prefers to do all of his intake work in person. With some of his patients."

She put the tablet down on her lap. "Patients like me, you mean. Court-ordered."

His eyes flicked away, not meeting hers. "Yeah. But he has a good reason. He likes to get to know people from the start. Talk about what's going on. He's a good therapist, I promise."

"He couldn't bother himself to be here tonight." She plucked the stylus from the side of the case and clicked on the first form.

"He's..." Cameron sighed. "Don't repeat this, but Matt's not great with the scheduling software. But he's really good at his job otherwise."

Sasha swallowed down the rising impatience as she clicked the cells on the form one by one. Typical, that she wouldn't receive the same treatment as other patients.

"I see. He needs to be here to talk to me about...my birthday. I'm twenty-five. Guess he needs me to tell him that in person. I'm an Aries, too."

Cameron's left eyebrow went up. "You believe in astrology?"

She lifted a shoulder. "It's more reliable than a lot of other systems."

He refrained from commenting further. He was probably judging her right now, because astrology wasn't scientific enough for him. She'd met guys like him before.

She scrawled her answers on the first few lines of the form, pressing too hard with the stylus. Irritation built inside her. All of this could have been an email. Every question. But she wasn't to be trusted with that task.

She drew in a breath, trying to calm herself enough to finish this paperwork and get out of here. This was better than the alternative. Better by far.

She looked up to find Cameron watching her in silence. The expression on his face had frozen, as if he'd started out focusing on her face, then lapsed into absentminded staring.

People stared at her a lot. The ink and piercings had that effect, and she was used to it, but she also had to call people out when it got too intrusive. Her annoyance kicked right back

17

into overdrive.

"I don't mean to be rude, but are you okay?" she asked.

"What?" He snapped to attention, yanking his gaze back to his laptop screen. "I'm fine."

"You were asleep when I got here, and just now, you zoned out again."

He passed a hand over his forehead. "I'm sorry. I think… I'm sorry. You caught me on a bad day."

"That makes two of us, then," she grumbled.

She spent a few more minutes filling out the questions on the sheet, all of it basic information. She flew through the medical history form, but stopped when she got to a longer form asking for more detailed answers.

"I don't know what to put here." Her words broke the silence, and Cameron's head came up.

"For what question?" he asked.

"It's asking why I'm seeking treatment here. Should I say, 'because I have to'?"

Cameron's brows lowered halfway. He seemed more awake now, his gaze sharper.

"I know that's part of your situation," he said. "That you were… That you have to be here. But I think the question is asking why you think you're here? What do you need to work on?"

It wasn't Cameron's fault that the question was perfectly worded to send her anger spiraling. A flush rose in her face, and her pulse hammered in her ears.

Why do you think you're here?

A question every person in authority liked to ask, every time she did anything out of line. From the assistant principal in high school down to her court-appointed attorney.

She blew out a breath and carefully set the tablet on the edge of the desk, because she didn't break expensive things. Not often, at least.

She stood, her leather jacket creaking as she crossed her arms over her chest. Time to make everything super clear for the over-tired admin assistant and the therapist who held her freedom in his hands.

"I'm here because a court ordered me to be here. I have to do anger management therapy, because according to them, I can't control my behavior."

She could control it, all right. She was controlling it right now, had spent a lifetime disciplining what Dad called her 'beautiful rages.'

And she'd been very in control the night she'd committed the crime that led to her being on probation right now. Destructive, but in control.

There was a long pause as Cameron processed the fact that she might be a violent criminal. He rose from his chair, matching her posture.

"I'm not going to ask you about your court case or what happened," he said slowly. "I'm not your therapist."

"I don't care who knows. I got in a fight, picked the guy up, used his body to smash a storefront, and got caught doing it on camera. Destruction of private property."

She gave an elaborate shrug, as if the sentence didn't sting every time she heard it. No one had asked her if her property had been destroyed.

For several minutes, Cameron appeared lost in thought again, his gaze unfocused. She'd shocked him. He'd probably never been in a fight in his life. Or maybe he was about to pass out.

"Are you okay?" she asked him, for the second time.

He shook himself back to attention. "Sorry. I'm really... That made me think of something else. It's a serious allegation."

"It's not an allegation. I did it. I was convicted on two counts, and I'm on probation now. I have to do anger management therapy and community service, or else I get thirty days in jail. Which isn't an option for me."

"I would like to know..." He stopped himself with a shake of his head. "No, it's none of my business."

"What were you about to ask?" She leaned forward, suddenly curious. It didn't matter what he wanted to know about her situation, because she wouldn't see him again after tonight, anyway.

His eyes went alert again, sharp with intelligence and curiosity. He looked like he had a lot more questions he was stopping himself from asking. He looked like he was actually paying attention to what she had to say. Which was something new.

"I was going to ask what the other guy did," he said, his tone wry.

Her breath stuck in her throat. The hot, pounding feeling in her head was back, but it wasn't anger this time.

No one had asked her that question first. No one had assumed she hadn't been spoiling for a fight from the start. Not in the whole process of the trial, sentencing, and legal paperwork she'd been through the last two months.

Sure, they'd wanted to know what "precipitated the attack." But she'd been the perpetrator in their eyes. Maybe because she hadn't bothered explaining the whole story of the last six months to them, the multiple incidents leading up to that night.

The camera hadn't caught the guy's face. It also hadn't

caught the start of their argument, or him throwing the first punch. She hadn't had any evidence to prove she'd acted in self-defense, and in the end, it was her and a broken-up storefront, facing the consequences.

As the defendant, she'd been forced in court to watch footage of herself picking up the asshole who'd vandalized her family's property and slamming him into the storefront window, shattering the glass, before he ran off and disappeared into the night.

No one else's first question had been about what was done to her.

Also to his credit, Cameron hadn't asked her something ridiculous, like how a woman could pick up a guy. Because then she might have had to demonstrate for him. The man in front of her was maybe six foot one, a buck seventy tops. Not a problem.

Adrenaline pulsed through her, making her hands curl into fists. After this appointment, she had a date with her punching bag at home. Where she would imagine the face of the asshole who'd spray-painted Dad's truck over and over.

"The other guy…" She let out a shaky exhale. "The other guy messed with my family. I'll leave it at that."

Cameron shifted on his feet. "Okay. I get that."

"Can we be done for tonight? I can call to reschedule my appointment tomorrow. I just…really want to be done."

This was the exact reason why she hadn't wanted to come to therapy. Digging into your feelings was a waste of breath. All it did was stir things up and make them worse.

"You don't want to finish your form?" he asked.

"I'll finish it next time. You told me Matt wants to go over all this information with me in person anyway."

She'd shown up here and done what she'd been ordered to do. It wasn't her fault that her counselor was incompetent. Or that his admin assistant was half dead on his feet.

It wasn't fair. She shouldn't be the one here. The asshole had gotten off free, of course.

Justice hadn't been served. But justice was a pretty word that applied to people who had the means to make the system work for them.

She took a few quick steps to the doorway, and Cameron made no move to follow her, frozen in place behind his desk.

"I remember where the door is," she told him.

She'd turned and had one foot on the staircase when he stopped her with a word.

"Wait."

She turned to face him. He rubbed the back of his neck, looking almost sheepish.

"I know you didn't want to come here," he said. "But I hope your therapy will be useful. I'm sorry about how you got introduced to the clinic. This isn't us at our best."

She swallowed. "It's okay. Happens to me all the time."

"And I guess…" He paused, his gaze shifting away from her. "I guess you'll tell Matt. About how you found me asleep in his office."

She tilted her head to the side, considering. She hadn't thought that far ahead, but now that he mentioned it, it would be pretty embarrassing for a guy like him, having his coworkers find out about how she'd found him tonight.

Cameron seemed like a nice enough guy. He'd listened to her, too. He hadn't judged her the second he saw her. For tonight, she'd give him a break.

"I don't need to tell him…probably," she added.

Chapter 2

She couldn't stop a grin at the shocked expression on his face. Yeah, she'd keep him in suspense. It was good for men to feel uncomfortable once in a while. For a change.

"Get some sleep," she told him, and gave him a mock salute before jogging down the stairs. He didn't follow.

As she shut the door of the clinic behind her, she gulped in breaths of the cold February air and headed to her car.

One session down, seven to go. Then she'd put this whole mess behind her.

Chapter 3

❦

Sasha's knife slid through the onions at top speed, her fingers gripping the handle with the ease of a lifetime of use. Her sinuses burned as the onion's tear gas filled the small space of the food truck. She had ten pounds of onions to dice first thing today before she moved on to potatoes.

A well-sharpened knife was a beautiful thing, making the simple task a joy. Working fast with a blade left no room for her mind to wander. Doing things was always better than thinking about things.

The door banged open behind her, letting in some welcome fresh air.

"Hey, Dad," she called over her shoulder.

"You're here early today." He started to draw the door shut behind him, then seemed to think better of it.

"Figured I'd get a head start."

No need to fill him in on her first therapy session last night and everything that short conversation with Cameron had brought up.

After going home last night, she'd whaled on her punching bag for a half hour, showered, and then watched TV until her eyes wouldn't stay open. Sleep was better than thinking, too.

This morning, all the thoughts came back, though. The memories from the night of her fight had popped up at random moments as she'd gone through her morning run and blended her protein shake. If this is what one not-even therapy session did, she'd have to brace herself for the next seven.

Damn talking and everything it brought along with it.

Cameron hadn't seemed to judge her, but even a few simple questions were too many. Even though he'd assured her that her real therapist was great at his job, it didn't mean she'd enjoy it. People in positions of authority were rarely helpful.

She scraped the last cutting board of diced onions into a plastic bin, then turned the heat on under the large skillet on the stove. Another pot with boiling water for the potatoes waited on the back burner.

Dad's heavy steps approached and he surveyed her as she swirled olive oil in the pan. He gave a nod of approval, then opened the storage cabinets to extract the flour bins. Dad never cried at the onion fumes anymore, even when the frying onions made her stick her head out the window. His sinuses had been scorched from decades of onion tears, and other kinds of tears, too.

He hoisted a forty-pound bag of flour onto his shoulder and tipped it into the bin, his movements sure and precise. He never spilled flour on the floor like she still did sometimes.

When her parents had moved here from Ukraine, he and Mom had worked their way up from selling knishes and bialys at farmers markets and fairs, until they saved up enough money to buy the food truck. But the truck was getting older now, its lavender paint peeling and patched over, the letters on the side halfway scratched off.

"I picked up the paper goods order today." Dad crumpled the flour bag in his fist and straightened. "And one more extra thing."

She dumped her first batch of onions into the hot oil and raised a brow at him. Dad's errands went like clockwork. He never deviated from the shopping list or the budget.

"What one more thing?" she asked.

"I'll go get it. Maybe the onions can wait a bit?" He sounded uncomfortable, and the strange tone of his voice made her gut clench. He never told her to stop cooking when she was in the middle of a task, either.

She shut off the burner and moved the pan off the heat.

He stomped out the door and returned a minute later, holding two iced coffees from the donut shop. He set them down on the dinette table at the front and gestured for her to come sit with him. The truck was a converted RV, so it had not only a full kitchen, but a dining area, and even a bed in the loft above the driver's seat.

"You got my favorite coffee." She grabbed a cup and took a long swig, trying to act casual. "What's the special occasion?"

"Don't you want to sit?"

She dropped into one of the chairs, now fully on alert.

"Thank you for coming early today." Dad studied his cup, which looked tiny in his massive hands.

The conversation was already getting weird. Dad never thanked her for coming, and she worked her unpaid morning hours like clockwork, five mornings a week.

"You know I'm glad to do it," she said.

"I don't want to make you late for your job."

"I've told you a hundred times, you don't make me late. My classes are all in the afternoons and evenings."

Her job teaching mixed martial arts and self-defense classes downtown paid the bills, but more than that, it made Dad proud of her. He'd been the one to enroll her in martial arts at age five. He'd worked all the extra hours to pay for those classes, too.

He took another sip of his coffee and watched her across the table. He hated iced coffee, but he'd gotten one to match hers.

"Dad, what's going on?" The words burst out of her. She didn't need any more bad news or surprises this week.

"I have something to run by you." He leaned back in his chair, resting his hands on the edge of the table.

Her stomach tightened. "They came back. Did you have trouble last night? You should have called me."

She hadn't seen any graffiti on the outside of the truck this morning, but that didn't mean something hadn't happened.

"No. No trouble last night. I closed up like normal," he reassured her.

"Then what?"

Dad twisted his cup around, peeling the paper label off with a fingernail. He looked more tired these days, but everyone in the neighborhood did. It was exhausting, keeping an eye out for criminals day and night.

Dad was the strongest man she'd ever known. Built like a bull, with a barrel chest, salt and pepper hair, and a square jaw. Still, she didn't like how thin the skin looked on his hands or the dark circles under his eyes.

"First of all, I want you to know this decision has nothing to do with your court case," he said. "I'm proud of you for doing what you thought was right."

Her spine went rigid. "Decision about what?"

He let out a heavy sigh. "I'm thinking about selling the truck, Sasha."

"What? No." She shoved her chair back and stood.

"I know it's not worth much now," he said. "But it will bring in enough money to last me for a while, while I figure out what to do next."

"What to do next?" she echoed. "You love this truck."

The truck wouldn't bring in enough money for Dad to live on for a year. And he didn't have enough saved up to retire.

"I do love it." His voice held a thread of uncertainty she didn't recognize. "But I just... I thought it might be time for a change."

She peered down at him, trying to read his expression.

"What brought this on? It *is* because of me, isn't it? You don't have to lie. I put a lot of stress on you this month."

The endless days in court for the trial flashed in front of her. Dad's grim face as they read the verdict and her sentence. She shouldn't have put him through all that.

His gaze shifted to the side. "I told you, it's not that."

She paced the length of the kitchen, all five steps in one direction and five steps back.

"I know you're not mad at me about it. But if you're thinking of selling, it's something to do with them. They've been back how many times this winter to graffiti the trucks? They're pushing you out. Don't let them, or they win."

Rage threatened to boil over inside her, lighting her veins on fire. It wasn't just their truck. The whole community had taken hit after hit over the last few months.

"Sasha, sit," Dad said, his voice weary. "I'm just tired of dealing with it. It doesn't seem worth it some days. I can paint over the graffiti a dozen times, and it still happens again—"

"I'll do the painting. Let me do that part. Call me whenever it happens." She dropped into her chair and put a hand on his forearm. "Maybe we can find a new place to move the truck to. A different neighborhood—"

He cut her off with a slashing gesture of his hand. "You know this is the best area in the city for food trucks. If we want to turn a profit at all, we have to stay here."

"We'll get new security cameras."

"And how many of those have we gone through already? Five? Seven? I've lost count."

No matter how many cameras they'd bought, they'd never caught any footage of the criminals. And the devices were always destroyed within days.

"Anyway, I told you it's not just that," he went on. "I've been doing this on my own for a while now. When Mom was here…" He broke off, shaking his head.

Mom had died twenty years ago, her memory only a shadow in Sasha's mind. But sometimes, for Dad, it was like she'd just passed last month.

"I'll help out more often," she promised. "I can reschedule some of my classes."

"No. Your classes are more important than an old food truck."

"Not to me."

He sighed. "You're a good daughter. But you know, eventually, I'll have to retire. Why not now?"

Because he didn't have enough money to retire, he was only fifty-seven, and she didn't have enough money to support him. And he damn well knew all of those things.

He was also the hardest worker she'd ever met. He'd never

29

once mentioned retirement. It didn't make sense he'd want to give up on the business now.

A sliver of unease shot through her. There was something else he wasn't saying. Maybe the truck was failing financially, or he was sick with something he wouldn't tell her about.

Or maybe he'd told her the truth. He was tired and lonely.

"I'll find you some extra help. Help you won't have to pay for," she rushed on when he looked about to protest. "Maybe some community volunteers. We'll support you. Can you keep going for a while longer while I figure out a way to make that happen?"

He rubbed a hand over his forehead, a gesture he only did when he was overwhelmed, either by emotion or exhaustion.

"Dad. It's going to be okay."

"You don't know that," he said, his words muffled by his hand. "And it's not your job to take care of this. You have your own life and problems. I can take care of mine."

But she'd added to his problems by getting herself arrested. A little knife twisted in her chest.

"It will be okay," she repeated. "I'm not sure what it'll take, but we'll keep trying different things. Besides, Mom wouldn't want you to sell the truck. Not yet, anyway."

It was an appeal to his emotions, maybe the one thing that could convince him to stop this crazy talk.

He dropped his hand and looked up at her, his eyes rimmed red. "It was her recipes that made all this happen, you know."

"I know. They're the best knishes in the world."

"She loved sharing them with people. Seeing them take their first bite. Then seeing the same people come back for more. She liked feeding people."

Sasha nodded, holding his gaze. "That's the best part."

Dad's chest rose on a long inhale. "Okay. I'll wait to make a decision."

Relief flooded her chest. "Good. That's good. We'll find a way to take some of the pressure off you. I promise."

"I'll be fine." He pushed his chair back with a scrape, his expression settling into a more familiar, stubborn expression. "Don't know what got into me, thinking like that. I'm going to unload the car."

A few minutes later, he'd stocked the truck. She watched as he pulled the car out of the parking space and went to deliver extra supplies to Anya, who owned the Nepalese momo truck across the square. They pooled orders for basic supplies and split the costs.

Sasha flipped the switch on the burner and put her hands on her hips while she waited for the oil to reheat. Taking deep breaths, she looked around the old truck, seeing it through a new lens. It was getting older, more shabby.

Everything got old and fell apart eventually. She just wasn't ready for it to happen yet.

* * *

By the time she made it to the gym, showered to get the onion smell out of her hair, and changed into workout clothes, it was after 1:00 p.m. When she opened the glass doors of The Women's Health and Fitness Center, and the smell of sweat, disinfectant, and rubber mats hit her nose, she calmed down a fraction. Even the fluorescent lighting was somehow comforting.

Her first class wasn't until 2:00, so she spent time warming up with her Tai Chi form. Her body went through the movements, which had a calming effect on a normal day.

Today was not a normal day. Her mind played the conversation with Dad on a loop. Something had been off in the tone of his voice, the expression on his face, when he'd suggested selling the truck. Something familiar, but in a way she couldn't pinpoint. She'd been too shocked at the words to analyze it at the time.

She moved through Brush Knee and Repulsing the Monkey, moving her feet backward across the gym mat. It hit her halfway through her form, what his face had been telling her subconscious mind.

Dad was scared. His expression had been familiar because it was the same expression the women in her self-defense class had sometimes, their first time coming into the gym. The women who'd been beaten or intimidated, and who looked uncomfortable taking up space in their own bodies.

The expression was so out of place on him because Dad wasn't scared of anyone. Maybe her arrest and court case had shaken him more than she'd realized. In the weeks leading up to her court date, he'd seemed different, subdued.

His current anxiety had to be because of her. So it was her responsibility to help him out more. She'd find volunteers to help him, check in on him at night before he closed the truck.

And maybe doing her anger management therapy—actually trying—would set his mind at ease.

She rolled her shoulders, flowing through the final set of movements in the form. A solid kickboxing workout would do more for her than talking about her problems with a therapist, who couldn't care less about her circumstances.

Chapter 3

Cameron had seemed to listen to her. But it would be dangerous to believe that meant she could open up to her therapist. Maybe she should try telling him the basics of her situation in her first real therapy session.

Or maybe she should shut up, keep her head down, and say the things they expected her to say. She cut through the final movements with a lot more violence than the gentle Tai Chi practice called for.

Maybe one day, she'd learn to think before she acted. But today was not that day.

Chapter 4

Cameron knocked on the door of Dr. Gold's office and waited until he heard his supervisor's voice through the heavy oak door.

"Come in."

He felt numb as he put a hand to the knob and turned it. He'd only given the new data sets a quick glance yesterday before shutting his laptop.

He couldn't do anything before talking to Gold, anyway. Any work he tried to do would be wrong in his advisor's eyes. So he'd waited forty-eight hours for this meeting and, for the first time in seven years, hadn't worked on schoolwork after work.

It had been…not relaxing at all.

Whatever people thought he should do when they suggested he take days off, he hadn't been able to do it. Sleep was never much of an option, and none of his old hobbies sparked any interest. When he wasn't at The Well Space, he'd parked himself on the couch and turned the TV on, so he appeared to be doing something. But he hadn't watched it.

Patients in his study had described the feeling of burnout in their surveys, and he'd read countless journal articles on the condition. Somehow, he'd assumed he could learn about it, but it would never happen to him.

Further proof of how far he'd let himself go was how badly he'd fumbled the intake session with Sasha the other night. On an ordinary day, he'd have been professional and competent. Instead, she'd seen him at his worst. Asleep. Wrinkled. Dropping things and forgetting words mid-sentence.

He'd also been distracted—by the ink trailing down the neckline of her T-shirt and disappearing under her collar. Apparently, the more tired he got, the harder it was to control his brain.

She hadn't promised not to tell Matt, either. About finding him asleep at the other man's desk. He cringed every time the memory surfaced.

She'd be within her rights to tell Matt. And Matt would tell Ben, who would then figure out how many extra late nights he'd been working. Each morning, he'd walked into work expecting to hear about it. But so far, no one appeared to know.

It wasn't just a matter of being embarrassed by his behavior. He'd be in trouble for this incident and for what it represented. His inability to do his own job.

He'd acted unprofessionally. He deserved whatever was coming his way from Ben. But he didn't need one more thing right now.

It appeared when your life went down in flames, it went all the way down in flames.

He sucked in a fortifying breath and entered the office of the world's biggest asshole, and also his advisor for the last year.

"Cam. Have a seat." Dr. Gold gestured to the leather chair across from his desk, and Cameron sat.

He'd long ago stopped correcting Dr. Gold about his name. No one called him Cam, and the sound grated on his ears.

"So. I got your email. About the data filtering." No sense wasting either of their time.

"Piece of bad luck, huh?" His advisor's mouth turned up at the corner, without managing to make him look the slightest bit more friendly.

Gold was young for a professor, maybe early thirties, with wavy, light brown hair brushed to the side and a square jaw. Clean-cut and always dressed in button-downs and chinos, he looked like he belonged at a yacht club, not a lab.

"I'm not sure how it happened," Cameron began.

He'd rehearsed this speech, in which he would bring up the possibility that this error was Gold's fault.

The older man steepled his fingers together. "I know how it happened. Carelessness."

"About that." Cameron cleared his throat. "I assumed you'd checked which participants were included in the study before I started working on the analysis."

Gold narrowed his eyes. "That was your job. You're the research lead on this study. This was your responsibility."

"But you—" Cameron drew in a careful breath. Arguing got you nowhere. Making the other person angry was pointless.

He should not point out, for example, that Gold had told him they'd collaborate on all the reports. That they would share them on the same drive. For all he knew, Gold might have changed something in one of the files without informing him.

He set his shoulders and looked straight ahead. "And the due date is still—"

"The date's not changing. April 15th."

The man's voice was calm—relaxed, even. He'd dumped all this extra work onto Cameron, and wouldn't even adjust the timing of the study.

He was right not to delay it. Graduation was in May. And he held Cameron's PhD research in his hands.

Cameron shut his eyes for a minute. When he opened them, Gold was watching him, a curious expression on his face. As if he had no idea how much added work he'd just piled onto his mentee.

"It'll be...a push to get those redone by April," he said.

Understatement of the year.

It would be a superhuman feat to reorganize every piece of data and redo every report. Impossible for most people. Maybe the old Cameron would have enjoyed the challenge.

"Well, hopefully you hadn't gotten too far in your analysis yet. For a guy who works as hard as you, this should be no problem. Right?"

"No problem," he echoed.

"Well, you've got your work cut out for you," Gold said, folding his arms across his chest.

A thoughtful expression crossed his face. "Of course, if it *is* taking longer than you thought, we'll need to extend your dissertation deadline. But that would push back your graduation—"

"I won't need an extension." Cameron rose from his chair in a rush. "I'll take care of it."

An extension would only prolong this agony.

"Good. You can let me know if you have any questions, of course."

Gold's tone did not invite questions, and every person who worked in the lab had learned a long time ago not to ask any.

"Of course."

He bobbed his head and made his escape from the stifling room. He jogged down the steps of the university research hall and out the front door.

If there was one thing that had always made him feel better about graduate school, it was that he could do any amount of work, put in superhuman hours.

When he was a kid, he'd pretend to be a robot to make his chores go faster. Mom wasn't up to making dinner? The robot could take care of that. No one had vacuumed the house? Another job for the robot. He could do any amount of work without caring about why, as long as he could separate himself from the tasks.

It was easier and safer to grind through work as the robot. People appreciated hard workers, though maybe they also took advantage of them.

He made it to his car, a decade-old silver hybrid, and slid inside. His breath came too fast, and he gripped the wheel with his hands. His calm, cool detachment slid out of place for a minute.

This was too much. Too much for one person. And he didn't care about it anymore. It brought no spark of excitement, or even interest, in his burnt-out state. The reasons he'd started grad school, his motivations for staying in it—all those things were nowhere to be found at this moment.

"I quit," he told the steering wheel. "I. Quit."

The words felt fantastic coming out of his mouth. Even if they were a lie.

He couldn't quit. He was too close to the finish line. He'd

come this far, so he'd have to keep going. Even though now, with the added weight of more work, the finish line seemed even farther away.

He couldn't quit. But maybe he could quit caring quite so much. Maybe, instead of giving a hundred and ten percent of his energy to his work, he could give twenty to thirty percent.

His dissertation would suck. But he didn't care anymore if it was sub-par. He was smart enough to make things up. Toss out some nonsense analyses and pass by the skin of his teeth.

Which seemed to be what a lot of other people around here did.

He put the car in drive and headed back downtown to The Well Space. He'd arranged this meeting on his lunch break, so now he hadn't eaten lunch, and it was time to get back to work. Which wasn't unusual for him.

What was unusual was him stopping at a coffee shop and getting an everything bagel with extra cream cheese, plus a scone for later. And an extra-large coffee. Later, at his desk, he'd skim through the new data. Figure out the least-effort way to go about this.

Like a true slacker.

His stomach clenched because this was dangerous behavior. The exact kind of thing he'd always avoided in the past. He'd seen where dangerous behavior got people and had never cared to participate.

But he didn't have a lot of options left. He'd have to do it this way or not graduate, and he'd choose to graduate. Everything he'd worked for had led up to this year. To the possibility of working full time at the clinic he'd started to feel was his second home.

Back at the office, Ben and Vanessa were waiting for him at

the top of the stairs. As the founding partners, the two of them met frequently to collaborate about the clinic, so it wasn't all that unusual to see them together upstairs. But the fact they were standing in front of his desk waiting was unusual.

"You took an actual lunch break," Ben said, giving an approving nod at the brown paper bag in his hand.

"I guess I did, for once."

Ben had gotten so serious about his employees taking better care of themselves. Cameron swallowed down his reflexive guilt at how much he hadn't been doing that.

As a new grad student, he'd idolized Ben, and when he'd gotten this admin assistant job, it had been a dream come true. He hated lying to his boss, much less not living up to the man's expectations for how his staff members should behave.

If Ben found out about the other night... He didn't want to think about it.

"Glad to see you taking the time," Ben said. His eyes scanned Cameron, as if he could see inside his head.

"Everything's going okay with school still?" Vanessa asked. She knew how many extra hours he'd put in lately.

He looked down at his shoes. "Fine. Lots of work, but I'm almost there."

These were the words you were supposed to say when people asked you about how school was going. You were not supposed to say you were slowly drowning, and you'd just decided to quiet-quit your dissertation.

"Well. Hang in there." Ben studied him for another beat.

His boss didn't smile much, but he wasn't rude, arrogant, and uncaring like Dr. Gold. He was also very perceptive about other people's emotions. Even when other people pretended not to have them as much as possible.

"You know," Ben said. "I've heard a rumor of a possible new therapist position opening up on the staff this summer."

Cameron froze, because of course it wasn't a rumor. If there was a new therapist position, it was because Ben had created one. A glance at the huge grin on Vanessa's face confirmed the fact.

"That sounds…like a pretty good opportunity." He tried hard to keep any hint of eagerness out of his tone.

This was what he'd been working toward. Why he hadn't taken a therapist position with another clinic after earning his Master's degree, and instead stayed on here as an admin assistant. He'd been waiting for this.

If he had to delay his graduation, this opportunity would be given to someone else. The Well Space needed more therapists at the rate they were growing.

"I've heard this is a great place to work," Vanessa said. "And there's an empty office next to mine."

A half smile curled Ben's mouth. "We'd give precedence to our own internal applicants, of course."

"Of course," Cameron echoed.

"Just something to keep in mind."

Ben went back into his office and shut the door, leaving Cameron standing by his desk with Vanessa.

She gave him a serious look. "You're still taking spring break off, like you promised me."

"How could I forget?" She'd caught him working late one too many times this month, and in exchange for her not telling Ben about it, she'd made him agree to actually be gone the second week in March. It wasn't like he could sneak in and work anyway because Ben would be here.

"I mean it, Cameron. Just because this is a golden opportunity doesn't mean you have to work yourself to the bone for it. I'd say you have a pretty good shot at getting it. Take care of yourself in the meantime."

She patted his arm and swished down the stairs.

A golden opportunity. In his three years working here, he'd hoped to hear those exact words. And now the job here was a real possibility, shimmering in front of him.

One more reason to push through and finish this semester. One more reason he couldn't stop now.

* * *

Four nights later, he was at his desk late again, speeding through creating a report without really looking at it, and high on a double-shot latte. If Ben knew he was here, he'd be in trouble, but this was the only way to make it happen.

He was typing near-nonsense. Made-up words that barely skimmed the surface of the analysis. He'd even flirted with the idea of using AI-generated text before tossing that plan. He wasn't that far out of his mind yet. Even if Gold didn't spot the regurgitated text from a mile away, they ran the dissertations through a checker. Getting thrown out of school for cheating was a step too far.

His brain was a machine, and he'd use it like one. Work fast, head down, and don't think about the consequences.

Shut everything out and do the job.

His hands paused on the keyboard at the sound of the front door opening. Because only one therapist on staff took patient appointments this late in the evening.

He hadn't let himself check the master schedule to find out when Sasha's new appointment was. But now his hand reached for the mouse and opened the calendar on autopilot. Confirmed what he already suspected.

Matt was meeting with Sasha tonight. She was downstairs right now.

His stomach dropped. Matt would find out what happened last time she'd been here. A week later, it seemed like a fever dream, something he'd made up. But it had been real.

And once she told Matt, and Matt told Ben, everyone would know the full extent of his fuckup. With the worst possible timing.

He should have told Ben today. He'd had a dozen opportunities to do it. But he didn't seem to be acting responsible these days.

Sasha was back, and she was about to blow up his world, which was already hanging on by a thread.

He should get up and leave right now. Go home, where he was supposed to be at this time of night anyway. But his body stayed put in the chair. Because she was downstairs, two floors below him. He would not sneak past Matt's door and escape into the night.

No, he would stay and face the consequences. He put his head down and focused on the report in front of him.

An hour later, the sound of footsteps on the staircase brought his head up.

Sasha appeared at the top of the stairs, eyes sharp and cheeks flushed. His breath stopped in his throat.

She was even more vibrant than he'd remembered, every part of her somehow more bright than her surroundings. The flash of silver at her nose and ears, the glossy dark hair. His brain hadn't exaggerated the memory of her brilliant ink and generous curves.

Or the fire in her unusual, color-swirled eyes. A fire that was currently directed at him.

"You and I need to chat," she said, folding her arms across her chest.

Chapter 5

Sasha watched as Cameron stood from his desk slowly, looking surprised and a little self-conscious. He shouldn't have been surprised, considering she was required to come here for the next two months. The real question was why he was still here after 7:00 p.m. It was none of her business, but it didn't seem like the other counselors had a habit of working this late.

"Come on in," he said. "You can sit if you want."

"I'd rather stand, thanks."

"Okay." He rubbed a hand over the back of his neck, an uncomfortable gesture she remembered from last time. "I hope your first real counseling session went okay?"

"It was fine."

Matt turned out to be a middle-aged man in khakis and a faded blue sweater, with graying hair, kind eyes, and pictures of his husband and kids all over the office. He was also terrible with technology, as Cameron had hinted, a fact confirmed when it had taken him several minutes to open her patient record on his laptop. He'd gone over the basics of the court-mandated therapy program with her and reviewed the forms she'd filled out last time.

He'd do all right. She could sit through six more sessions with Matt, no problem. Even if she wasn't sure about telling him anything meaningful in the process.

"And you told him you were coming upstairs after your appointment because…"

"I said I wanted to thank you. For meeting with me last time."

"Ah." Cameron shifted on his feet, looking even more ill at ease. "Then you told him…uh. About how you found me."

"I didn't tell him, actually."

His gaze snapped to hers. "You didn't?"

"Nope. I told him you were working late that night, and you gave me my forms to fill out. That's it."

An uncertain expression crossed his face. He was probably wondering why she'd kept that information to herself. A question she'd asked herself more than once in the last hour.

"About that night," he said. "I owe you an apology. I was really out of it, and I wasn't acting like normal."

"I could kind of tell."

"And you'd be within your rights to tell Matt about my unprofessional behavior. I deserve it. It was really… That was not how I usually am."

She cocked her head to the side. "Aren't you going to ask me why I didn't tell him?"

"I was wondering."

She took a couple of steps closer to him. Almost into his personal space, but not quite. He was so much taller than her, she had to tip her head back to look at his face. His suspenders today had microbes printed on them, and a dark shadow of black stubble covered his chin. He smelled like coffee and worn-in aftershave.

"Because I wanted to talk to you again one more time before I decided what to do about it," she told him.

She'd had to see if what she remembered about him from last time was right. That he seemed to listen. Before she asked him the huge favor she was about to ask.

His eyebrow went up. "You should tell them about what happened. I'll deal with the fallout."

"I think you really would."

Other guys would make excuses to get out of trouble, rather than accept the consequences of their actions. Another guy would have lied to his coworkers and told them she'd exaggerated her account. Or straight up pretended it didn't happen and gaslit her about it.

He'd paid attention the other night. And now he was taking responsibility for his actions.

"You don't have much of a self-preservation instinct, do you?" she asked. She couldn't help poking at him a little bit, trying to figure out if he was for real.

"What do you mean?"

"You're throwing yourself under the bus."

He lifted a shoulder. "I messed up. In a very embarrassing way. I mean, not that I *want* them to find out. I've never done anything like that at work, and I'll never hear the end of it. My boss will not enjoy hearing the news, either. But at this point, it's just one more thing in the dumpster fire that is my life."

She leaned forward. "What would happen if your boss found out?"

"Nothing good." He cleared his throat. "He's really into his employees' health and well-being. Which makes sense, considering what we are." He waved his hand around, indicating the clinic in general.

"Huh. That's unusual."

"I know. But I don't want to be on his radar right now, if I don't have to."

"So you'd rather I not say anything," she pressed. "If you had a choice."

"If you wanted to keep quiet about it, I wouldn't object."

Triumph filled her, because she was about to get what she wanted. Everyone had a weak spot you could leverage. Now was the moment to ask. Cameron appeared to be one of the rare good guys in the world. He'd say yes.

"I won't say anything," she told him, "as long as you do me a favor."

His eyes sharpened. "A favor?"

"Yeah. I need help with something. And in exchange for your help, I'll stay quiet about your Sleeping Beauty performance the other night."

A dull red flush stained his cheeks.

"I see." He took a step back from her, caught his shoe on the edge of the rug, and stumbled.

She reached out her hand to help steady him automatically. Wiry muscles flexed under the cloth of his dress shirt. He was lean, but stronger than he looked. His hands were also shaking.

She flicked a glance at his desk. "How many of those coffees have you had today?"

He drew himself up straight, brushing a hand down his shirt. "Five. I think."

Her brows shot up. "Five coffees."

48

"I'm averaging three hours of sleep on a good night. Did you really just say I owe you a favor? Like some kind of mafia don?"

A laugh forced its way out of her. "You make it sound like I'm blackmailing you."

"Are you?" His eyes searched her face, and some of her usual attitude melted away under the examination. Unexpectedly, she found herself wanting to share the truth with him.

"No. Of course not. I just… There's something I need help with, and I thought this might be one way to get it."

"You could try a simple ask for help. Without anyone owing you a favor."

She snorted. "That sounds like something a counselor would say." But it wasn't the way the world worked, in her experience.

"I am a counselor. Or I will be soon, after I graduate this spring." He propped a hip on the edge of his desk. "So tell me what you need. Maybe I can help."

She shook her head because that was way too good an offer to be true. People didn't say things like that and mean it. She needed to get the upper hand back on the conversation.

Still, she couldn't shake the feeling he was interested in her point of view. That he cared and listened. Damn, counselors were scary in their own way.

Cameron's hand went to his brow again. It was shaking more than it had been a minute ago. He looked a shade paler, too.

"Do you need to sit down?" she asked.

"Yeah. I think… That would be good."

He crossed the space to his desk and sank into the chair. Without thinking, she went behind the desk and stood next to him.

Maybe she'd pushed him too hard, and now he was about to faint. Or maybe he'd had too much caffeine and not enough food.

"Did you eat anything else besides coffee today?" she demanded.

"Uh. I don't remember."

"Fuck's sake." She dug around in her shoulder bag for a protein bar. When she found one—the expensive kind, no less—she shoved it into his hand.

"Eat before you pass out. And drink your water." She nodded toward the full metal tumbler on his desk as he ripped open the protein bar and took a bite.

"I do know about hydration," he grumbled.

"Doesn't look like it to me. What are you doing, working so late all the time, anyway? I'd think an admin assistant wouldn't have such long hours."

"Like I said. Grad school." He polished off the last of the protein bar. "Thanks for that. I do usually manage to feed myself."

"Uh-huh." She peered over his shoulder at his laptop screen, which was filled with a complex, color-coded spreadsheet. "So that's your schoolwork?"

"Yep." He slid a hand to the laptop lid and clicked it shut. "But I don't want to look at it anymore tonight."

He folded his arms over his chest, leaning back in his chair. In that position, his legs looked a mile long. He'd rolled up the sleeves of his dress shirt again, revealing his forearms. If he ate and slept more, he could gain muscle, though he'd never be a beefy guy.

"So, either you need help, or I owe you a favor. I definitely owe you at least a protein bar now."

"Not the cheap kind, either," she told him.

"Of course. And what else do you need?" The last sentence came out softer, not judging her, not angry.

His eyes were so thoughtful, not clouded by suspicion or ego. He didn't seem to lead with his emotions. If she was facing him in a fight, she'd be worried, because people who could strategize without giving into their anger were powerful enemies.

She'd never had one as an ally.

"I think… What I need help with is…" She paused, the words not finding their way out of her mouth.

This was so much more than explaining her anger issues to a counselor. This was telling a real person her troubles and asking for help.

He leaned forward, elbows on his armrests. "You can tell me. I'll let you know if it's something I can help with or not."

She met his gaze, sucked in a breath, and told him the truth she hadn't told anyone.

"My dad's food truck business is struggling. We've been vandalized at least once a week, sometimes more, for months. He can't keep up with it. He's talking about quitting now, and I told him I'd find some volunteers to help him out for a while."

Cameron's brows went down. She could almost see the gears turning behind his eyes.

"I'm assuming he's reported the vandalism," he said.

Of course he thought the authorities would solve everything.

"Yeah, he's reported it. Not that it's done any good."

"I see." More processing. "So he reported it, the authorities didn't help, and it's something you're continuing to deal with."

"That's about it."

He met her eyes, assessing her. "And I'm guessing this has

something to do with your…your charges."

She gave a quick nod. "You'd be right."

She wasn't ashamed of what she'd done, but people tended to view you differently when they knew you'd been convicted of a crime.

"Well. I'm not an expert in criminal justice, of course. Matt's going to be your best bet for someone to help with the legal system. With your situation."

She shook her head. "I don't want to work with the legal system. I want as far away from the courts as I can get. I want volunteers there helping my dad." She squared her shoulders, letting the rest of her words fly. "I want him to stop looking over his shoulder all the time. He's been through enough this year. He needs help, not more legal processes. I work mornings before he opens, but I don't think that's enough anymore."

She tried to shake off the strange feeling she'd had, when Dad mentioned retiring, but it slithered through her gut again. The scared look on his face was still with her a week later.

But she'd been ridiculous, coming here to ask for help from a near stranger. Another wrongly placed hope—

"I used to work in a restaurant as an undergrad," Cameron said.

Her gaze flew to his, disbelieving.

"And I'm on spring break the week after next," he went on. "I could volunteer for a week. If that would help."

"You'd do that?" She could barely catch her breath. Now she was the one who needed to sit down. "Why would you give that much of your time?"

When she'd come here, she'd thought maybe he could be talked into an afternoon. But a whole week…

An uncomfortable look crossed Cameron's face. A combination of guilt and exhaustion.

"I don't mind helping out," he said. "I think…I might need something else to focus on other than school for a few days. And I'm being forced to take the time off from work, too."

"Forced into taking a vacation, huh?"

He shook his head. "You have no idea. It's been difficult for me to take time off the last few years. I'll need something to do with myself that week so I don't go crazy."

She scanned his face, looking for signs of insincerity, that he was yanking her chain. But he was serious.

Dad needed help. This would buy him a week of time, where he could explore other options, like new security cameras, or hiring another person part time—a suggestion he'd rejected in the past.

"Thank you," she said. "I didn't expect this much of your time."

Cameron snorted a laugh.

"What?"

"You have no idea how many unpaid hours I've worked for school. A week's not that much time to give."

"It means a lot to me. And Dad. He's stubborn about accepting help, but if it's okay with you, I'll tell him you need volunteer hours for school. It'll make him feel like he's doing you a favor, when it's the other way around."

He cocked his head. "You have a lot of tricks up your sleeve."

She smiled up at him. "Gotta size up your opponent. Know what you're dealing with."

"I see. You had me pretty well summed up." He stood from his desk and held out a hand for her to shake. "I'll plan to help out for a week."

"Deal." She shook his hand, which was warm and strong in hers. He was really not at all what she'd expected. "I'll text you the address and meet you there Monday morning after next."

After exchanging numbers, she jogged down the steps before he could change his mind. One volunteer for one week was a start.

Chapter 6

Eight days later, Cameron pulled his car into the paid downtown lot that Sasha had texted him the address for and pondered his life. He'd spent the last week speeding through the creation of some new data figures for the study, working on autopilot. The data were full of holes. Doubtless he'd made mistakes. And he was finding it hard to care, which was a bad sign.

And now he was spending half of his spring break working in a food truck. Sasha hadn't even told him what food the truck sold, or what he'd be doing to help out. Just an address and a time to show up.

He hadn't lied to her about needing an escape from schoolwork, though. He'd been forced to take the week off work, and if he stayed in his apartment and looked at data all week, he really would throw his laptop out the window.

The solution that made the most sense was to focus on something else, at least for part of the day.

You wouldn't have offered to help anyone else like this.

His interest in Sasha didn't make much rational sense. He did owe her a favor for not telling Matt about their disastrous meeting. At the least, he should do something to make the situation right. But a week's worth of volunteer time was possibly more than the situation called for.

Something about Sasha tugged at him and wouldn't let go. He'd lay money on the fact that she didn't ask for help easily, and didn't open up and tell strangers about her problems. But she'd done that with him. Not with her actual counselor.

People who didn't like to share their problems often had reasons for being that way. Maybe she'd been hurt or had her needs ignored in the past. It could have happened a thousand different ways, and for some reason, he wanted to know why. He would chalk it up to therapist curiosity. And not the fact that he was attracted to her.

He wouldn't act on the feeling. This was the worst possible time in his life to get involved with someone, not that it had ever been a good time in the last seven years.

But he could try to help her family out. With volunteer workers to take some of the pressure off her dad, they could focus on the bigger problem of the vandals who'd damaged their truck. He could do that much and walk away after this week knowing he'd helped in some small way.

He scanned the area before getting out of his car. The spacious square, lined with pear trees, was empty this time of morning, the parking areas wide open. Along the sides of the brick street in the renovated area of downtown stood rows of food trucks, most quiet and unoccupied.

He unfolded himself from his car and brushed a hand down his front. He hadn't worn work clothes, because if this was anything like working in a restaurant, he'd be covered in food by the end of the day. He'd chosen dark jeans and a yellow Henley, hoping it was the right option.

He took a shortcut across the square. She'd told him it was the only purple truck in the lot, and as soon as more trucks came into view, he spotted it.

The truck was more of a bright lavender, with white block lettering on the side. As he got closer, he made out the words: *Knishes and Bialys*.

The side door of the truck cracked open, and Sasha's head popped out. She looked happy to see him, and a lot less tense than she'd been in the clinic. She'd tied her short hair up in a tiny ponytail at the back of her head. Her face, free of makeup, looked younger with her hair up. The style also revealed rows of piercings in each ear, which had been hidden before.

"You made it," she told him.

"Yep." He shoved his hands in his pockets so he wouldn't stare at her. "So. Knishes."

"Hope you like onions." She grinned at him and opened the door the rest of the way, gesturing for him to come inside.

He followed her, taking two big steps up into the truck, a converted RV.

"You're not going to believe this. But I've never eaten a knish."

She rounded on him. "Never? Well, they can be hard to find in town. But that's about to change this morning, in about"—she checked her smartwatch—"three hours. Give or take, with the baking time."

"Sounds good." He stumbled over the end of the last word, because now that he was inside, he realized two things. One, the space was small, and they'd be working together alone.

And two, she wasn't wearing her jacket today, so he could

see her entire upper body. She had on her usual ripped jeans, a white tank top, and a pale blue apron tied around her waist. Her curves belonged in a museum, and her arms were works of art, inked up and down with bright colors he should definitely not stare at right now.

He looked down at his shoes, then over at the kitchen workspace, anywhere but at her.

He cleared his throat. "So, I guess show me what to do."

"I'll grab you an apron." She frowned down at him, not moving yet. "You're not wearing suspenders."

"I don't wear them every day. Only to work."

"You look like a normal person now."

"Glad to hear it," he said, his tone dry.

"I didn't mean I don't like them. They're very…old fashioned?"

"That's what people tell me." He didn't need to explain his fashion choices to her, or the fact that once he'd been perceived as a nerd all his life, he'd decided to lean into it, rather than fight it.

"Well. Come on back. I'll give you a tour."

He crossed the space to the back of the truck, which had been remodeled into a professional kitchen. The convection oven was familiar, as were the prep table, stainless steel dish sink, and drying racks.

"This is the kitchen." She gestured toward the back with one hand. "Up front's the sales area. That window rolls open, and that's where customers line up. We open at 11:00 a.m. for lunch, and close at 8:00. We're open until 11:00 p.m. on weekends."

"Long hours."

She nodded. "Yep. Dad and I tag team to get everything

done. I do the prep work in the mornings. I get here before Dad and get everything ready. I start baking at 10:00, and then at 11:00 or 12:00, I go to work, and he takes over for the rest of the day."

"You have another job?"

"Yeah, this isn't my full-time job. I teach martial arts at a women's gym."

That would explain how she'd felt confident enough to fight a man who had to have been bigger than her. Even if it didn't explain her motivations.

"What type of martial arts do you teach?" he asked.

"Tae kwon do, tai chi, and self-defense classes for women." She flashed a grin at him. "I love teaching people to fight. My gym is only open to people who identify as women, and we're really focused on building those skills so they don't have to feel threatened."

"It sounds like a good place."

"It is." She smiled again, showing all her teeth this time. He was having a hard time not getting pulled into that smile, because it was so different from the version of her he'd seen at the clinic. There, she'd been closed off, almost confrontational. Here, she seemed relaxed and happy, and seeing this other side of her made his brain spin.

He cleared his throat. "So you work two jobs, basically."

"Well, Dad doesn't pay me. He'd never hire help because he's a stubborn old man who thinks he can do everything himself," she said fondly. "But that's why you're here. You're going to help him without him realizing that's what's happening."

"So volunteers are okay, but paid help isn't?"

She cocked her head to the side. "Like I said, I'm gonna tell him you need the volunteer hours for school. That way, he can't say no. But someday, I hope I can convince him to hire someone else."

"So. Knish rolling." She reached around him and opened a narrow closet door, and he sucked in a breath as she brushed up against him. He had a brief impression of warm skin and a floral scent before she pulled away, holding an apron. "Step one is wash your hands and put this on. Lots of flour today."

"Got it." He shook his head to clear it and tied the white cotton apron around his waist.

When he'd washed his hands, he returned to the work space, where Sasha had lined up a plastic food storage tub of what looked like mashed potatoes alongside a bowl of bread dough covered with plastic wrap.

"The basics." She ripped off the plastic wrap and punched the dough down. "Do you know what a knish is?"

"I know what it is. I've just never had one."

"So you know it's potatoes inside bread dough. Carbs inside of carbs. Classic Eastern European Jewish food." She turned the bowl upside down, releasing the dough onto the countertop. "The recipe we use was my mom's. My parents moved here from Ukraine before I was born."

"Your parents are Jewish?"

"Dad isn't, Mom was. She died when I was five."

"I'm sorry."

"Don't be. I don't remember her well. But I ate a lot of her food growing up, because of the recipes she left."

"We have that in common—the one Jewish parent thing. My dad's Jewish and my mom's family is Scottish. But I wasn't raised practicing many Jewish traditions."

She put her hands on her hips, regarding him. "Me neither. It's weird, being half one thing and half another, but not really either, you know?"

"I know the feeling well." Too well, in a lot of parts of his life, not just his Jewishness. He'd been half nerd, half normal guy. Half human, half machine.

"Anyway, at least you got the food," he told her. "I didn't even get that much." Dad worked too many hours to cook, and Mom hadn't been up to it most days.

She pointed a finger at him. "That's all about to change, my friend. This is the food of your heart, you just don't know it yet."

He let out a half-laugh. "I'm not sure any food is the food of my heart. I'm more of an 'eat because I have to' kind of person."

He had to eat to keep on being alive. There wasn't a lot of joy in the process, only physical necessity.

She made a tsking sound and turned to the counter. "Just wait. Okay, this is the dough. And that's the filling. There's an art to wrapping these, which you're not going to get right on the first try."

"I wouldn't think so."

"So I'm going to roll out the dough and cut it. Watch where I score the lines. I'll have you put the filling on top. Then I'll show you how to wrap them. Watch and learn, Jewish food novice."

It was not a surprise Sasha was bossy in the kitchen, that she manhandled the dough into a large rectangle covering most of the countertop. She wasn't tall, so she had to stand on her tiptoes to leverage her weight into the rolling pin.

He got distracted again, mesmerized by her strong arms working the dough into four directions. Her ink drew his gaze, and he allowed himself to study it for a moment while

61

she wasn't looking.

A dragon on her left bicep, with a spiked tail coiling around her forearm. A stylized ocean wave and a large floral design. On her left wrist, some lettering in the Cyrillic alphabet and the Hebrew alphabet, neither of which he could read. College friends had teased him for learning Klingon and Elvish when he could have applied himself to learning an actual global language.

The click of the rolling pin stopped, and he looked up to find her eyes on him. Caught.

"You like tattoos?" she asked, arching a brow.

"I was just… I wanted to look at them more closely," he admitted.

"You can ask me about one of them, then we're back to knishes."

"What does it say?" he asked, pointing to the scrolling letters wrapped around her wrist.

"It's my mom's name. In Ukrainian and Hebrew."

"What was her name?"

She shook her head. "I said one question. Maybe if you get a lot done this morning, I'll answer another."

"Unbelievable."

"I know you're curious about them. But you're here to help *me*, not the other way around. So I'm using your curiosity to my advantage."

"You do that a lot, don't you?"

"Do what?"

"Try to figure out what people want, and then use it."

"Of course." She shrugged. "It's called sizing up your opponent."

"I hope I'm not your opponent."

She raised a brow at him. "A week ago, I'd have said you were. Now, I'm undecided. Anyway, take this."

She shoved what looked like a tiny ice cream scoop into his hand.

"Put balls of the filling here, and here. Two inches apart, between the lines."

Precision was something he could do. Eyeing the lines she'd made in the dough rectangle, he created an identical row of filling balls.

She gave a nod of approval. "Good. You pay attention. Keep going."

She was strict about this procedure, which made sense, since her family had been making this recipe the same way forever. But also, he got the sense she liked ordering him around.

When he'd finished the task, she moved the filling bowl aside.

"Okay, now we fold. Believe it or not, people have big opinions about the shape of knishes, and what they should look like."

"I could see that being true. People are used to their favorite foods looking a certain way."

"Exactly. So when my parents started this business, they used my mom's recipe. But she wanted to do something different with it. Put her own twist on it. So what I'm about to show you is a top-secret family technique."

Using a bench scraper, she cut the dough into rectangles, gathered the corners together, pinched, and then twisted them in a smooth, practiced motion. The resulting pastry was round, with a twist of dough at the center.

"Now you." She gestured to the board in front of him, and he tried to repeat her motions.

"Not bad. Make sure you seal the edges better next time."

After several tries, with her correcting him each time, he fell into a rhythm. It was peaceful in the small space, cutting, pinching, and twisting dough in a repetitive motion.

They folded pastries in silence for a few minutes, Sasha checking over his shoulder to make sure he was doing it right. He hadn't worked with his hands like this for years, away from a computer screen for longer than an hour.

After they'd finished rolling the first batch, they transferred them onto baking sheets and began the process over again.

"Can I ask you something?" she said, a few minutes into the next batch. "Since you got to ask me a question."

"Go for it. I'm not as stingy with answers as you are."

She chewed on her bottom lip, thinking. "The night we met. Why weren't you bothered by me having a record?"

He stopped folding and faced her. "Why would I be?"

"A lot of people are. They find out you have a criminal record, and they treat you differently."

"Well, they shouldn't. And to answer your question about why, first of all, I don't make a habit of judging any of the clinic's patients. And second of all, I have a family member who's been in and out of jail. My older brother Robbie."

"Oh." Surprise and curiosity played across her face. She wanted to ask more, but she wouldn't. He'd spent his whole childhood dodging people's curious not-questions.

"It's not a secret, or something I want to hide. I've learned that when people don't talk about issues like this, it only increases the social stigma around them. Robbie is an addict. It's not his fault, and he's been fighting it his whole life. It's led to some legal problems for him, some of them unjustified. And some of them justified."

"I'm sorry," she said. "I wouldn't have guessed. You seem like you have your life together."

"But that's the thing. It can be anyone's family member or friend. That's why I don't judge."

"Anyway." He turned back to folding the knishes, to give his hands something to do. "He's in a good place in his life right now, sober and working a job he likes. So it's not a tragedy. It's what life dealt him."

She stood with her hip against the counter, watching him work for another long minute.

"What?" he asked, to break the silence.

She shook her head. "Nothing. I guess you surprised me again. You're so matter-of-fact about all this."

"I'm matter-of-fact about everything." He pinched the dough shut one last time and gestured to the neat row of perfect pastries. "Including knish-folding technique and psychological evaluations."

His stomach tightened for a moment because he had not been so motivated to do a good job with school in the last week. He'd been doing a half-decent job, fueled by caffeine and not caring. Being here this morning reminded him what it felt like to care about doing a good job.

He pushed away thoughts of his research. He was here helping out for a week to escape that reality.

Sasha reached across him and adjusted the edge of one of his pastries. "These aren't bad at all. But they're not as good as mine, of course."

Chapter 7

S asha eyed Cameron across the dining table in the truck. After they'd rolled out three hundred knishes, she'd preheated the oven, promising to make the first batch so they'd be done before he left.

He'd surprised her this morning, and not just with his above-average knish folding. He was a hard worker. At the clinic, he seemed all business, and she'd assumed he'd been born privileged and never worked physically in his life. But he'd proved her wrong.

He'd also been open about his family's problems in a way she never was with strangers. She hadn't expected him to answer her question with that much honesty. His brother's criminal record wasn't a tragedy in his view. So maybe hers wasn't, either.

She opened the fridge and handed him a cola. Fully loaded with sugar, because Cameron could use the calories. Cameron cracked the can and took a long drink. The scent of onions and browning dough filled the truck, and the small space heated up from the ovens.

"Three minutes until your life is forever changed," she told him, after checking the progress of the pastries through the oven window.

He looked dubious. "If you say so."

Five minutes later, she dropped a paper plate with two knishes in front of him on the table. Steam rose off the golden brown pastries.

"Do you have a fork?" he asked.

"We do not eat this with a fork." She dropped into the chair across from him, putting her own plate in front of her. "We eat it like this."

She picked up the hot pastry, blew on it to cool it, and took a big bite. Across from her, Cameron did the same. He froze, his eyes widening as he chewed.

"It's really good," he said around the mouthful of food.

"I told you."

He didn't raise a skeptical brow at her this time. He was too busy downing the rest of the food in a few bites. And maybe he wasn't a huge food person, but he looked to be enjoying this more than the protein bar. There was hope for him yet.

After he'd polished off the second knish, his eyes flicked to the tray on the stovetop.

"You want another?" she asked.

"No, I'm good."

"I think you could put away one more."

She got a third knish, dropped it on his plate, and went to start the dishes. From the corner of her eye, she saw him eat the third pastry in a few bites before quickly pushing his chair back and coming to help her.

With two people, the work had gone faster this morning.

Tomorrow would be even quicker, now that he knew what he was doing. They could get ahead on prep, maybe even get a few days' work done in advance. Dad could be so much less stressed…if only he had regular extra help like this.

After they'd finished the cleanup, she walked him to the door, and they both squinted outside in the bright sunshine.

"Thanks for coming today," she said.

"I'm glad I could help." Cameron shoved his hands in his pockets. He still looked tired, but he looked more relaxed than when he'd arrived.

"Maybe you'll take a nap this afternoon."

He snorted a laugh. "Not likely. But this was good. A good break for me. I appreciated getting away from the computer. I'll see you tomorrow, then."

He gave her a wave and headed toward the parking lot. She watched him walk across the square, long strides eating up the distance. People rarely surprised her, but Cameron had today, with his hard work, but also with his practical worldview that didn't see people like her as a problem. Most men she'd known were quick to make assumptions, never admitted they were wrong, and never saw things from another person's point of view.

She could almost see herself being friendly with him. Not something she'd ever experienced with a man. Men were good for a quick, fun time, and nothing more. Best kept at arm's length, where they couldn't do any damage. Which was the safest place to keep Cameron as well.

Twenty minutes later, Dad's car pulled into the alley behind the food trucks, his usual spot for unloading. He backed in and popped open the trunk, and she went to help him carry the week's grocery order in.

He stopped in his tracks when he stepped into the truck.

"You're already done with cleanup."

Of course he'd notice the slightest difference in the routine.

"I had a helper this morning. I showed him the ropes, and we got through everything a lot faster than usual."

Dad dropped the forty-pound bag of flour onto the counter. "A helper?"

"A volunteer. I told you I would find a way to support you more, and I'm trying something new. He needs volunteer hours for school, anyway."

Dad frowned. "He better have washed his hands."

"I made sure he washed his hands."

"And it's a man, eh. Where did you meet this man?"

She waved his question away. "The important thing is we're working on ways to get you help, so you don't feel so overwhelmed."

Dad's face hardened. "I'm not overwhelmed. Forget what I said the other day. Like I told you, I'm not sure what got into me."

He turned and stomped down the steps to the truck, heading back to his car.

She followed on his heels. "I won't forget it, because you've never said anything like that to me before. It made me think something's wrong."

Dad paused in the act of opening his car door, his hand resting on the roof. With his back to her, he let out a loud sigh.

"I wish you wouldn't worry about me."

He pulled out a large box from the wholesale store, brimming with groceries, and set it on the ground next to his feet. He extracted a twenty-pound burlap bag of rice from the back seat and shoved it into her arms.

"We're taking these to Anya."

He slammed the car door shut and picked up the box. She followed him across the square to the momo truck, an older, green trailer. Anya had sold the curry-filled dumplings here for the past three years. Dad picked up groceries and supplies for her, and in exchange, on busy Saturdays, her teenage son Kiran helped Dad out for a couple of hours.

It would affect more people than Anya if Dad sold the truck. He helped so many others in the community, many who were immigrants like him. He remembered what it was like to get started here, and he'd always paid it forward.

As she followed his broad back, the sense that something wasn't right persisted. But Dad had never been much of a talker.

He set down the box outside the momo truck and rapped on the door. The scent of curry and cumin wafted from the open windows. A moment later, the door cracked open, and Anya poked her head out.

"Alexei, come on in."

Anya wore a white apron tied over her yellow floral tunic, her shiny, dark brown hair tied back at the nape of her neck in a long ponytail. She was a few years younger than Dad, somewhere between forty and fifty. She was perspiring lightly, her medium brown skin glowing from the heat of the truck.

Dad hefted the box up once more and brought it inside. A moment later, he reappeared, took the bag of rice from Sasha's hands, and brought that inside, too.

Anya turned to Sasha, looking exasperated. "Your dad won't let me pay him for gas. Only the groceries."

"Sounds like him," she said.

The older woman shook her head. "He's stubborn. Doesn't

like to take anything extra in return."

"Thanks for letting Kiran help him out. He doesn't want to tell me he needs extra help on the weekends, but he does."

"He does." Anya gave a knowing nod, glancing over her shoulder into the truck. "And he won't stop working, even for one second. Even now, he's adjusting my oven door. I told him it wasn't closing right. Alexei, you don't have to do that now."

"It will only take a minute." Dad's voice drifted out from inside the truck.

Anya rolled her eyes and folded her arms across her chest. She glanced over her shoulder again, making sure Dad was still busy inside. She was taller than Sasha, and she bent at the waist so her voice landed closer to Sasha's ear.

"Ever since he chased those bad ones away from my truck, he's had nothing but trouble. I feel terrible about it, but what can I do?"

The hairs on Sasha's neck rose. "When did that happen?"

"About a month ago. A new group of boys came to bother me at night. I was packing up and getting ready to go home, and they followed me to my car. I told your dad I was scared, and he came and closed up with me every night for a week. Then one day they showed up and he threatened to call the police. So now they make extra trouble for him, too."

Sasha's hands curled into fists. "I'm glad he stayed with you."

Anya's brown eyes softened. "Me too. But I'm sorry for his trouble now. And yours."

Her kind, compassionate gaze was almost too much. Sasha cleared her throat. "He didn't tell me."

"He wouldn't. Oh, here he comes now," she added, raising her voice as Dad ducked out of the truck. "We were just talking about how stubborn you are."

Dad grunted and folded his Swiss army knife back into his pocket.

"Let me know if the door comes loose again," he said.

"I will. I'd better get in there and stir the chicken. Sasha, stop by on your way out for momos."

"Will do."

She followed Dad back to the truck, taking two steps for every one of his. She should take some time to think this through, think about how she would approach this conversation with Dad. But she'd never been very good at waiting to approach difficult subjects.

"So. Anya told me you'd had trouble with the vandals before. At her truck?"

Dad kept on walking, his back to her.

"She was getting harassed. I helped."

"But that's when they started targeting our truck more often."

"Yes."

She hurried along beside him, heart pounding. "What else happened that I don't know about? You said the whole neighborhood was going bad, that this was happening to everyone. But they're targeting us specifically, right?"

Dad stopped at the door to the RV, pausing with his hand on the knob. His shoulders sagged. "Yes. They're after me now. Instead of her. Which is a good thing, in many ways."

"And you didn't think it was important to tell me that tiny detail."

"Sasha, I… There are things you don't understand."

He shook his head and climbed into the truck. She followed right behind him. He should know better than to think she'd let go of this subject.

72

"Make me understand. What else is going on?"

She crowded into his space, tugging on his sleeve until he turned to face her. His face was stony, a wall in place in front of his eyes. His usual tired expression had turned guarded.

Her face flamed as anger threatened to consume her. "It's always been you and me. A team. But if you can't tell me what's happening, I'm not a part of the team."

"You don't understand," he repeated, raising his voice for the first time in the conversation. Good. His anger was better than the wall he'd put up a minute ago.

"You think I'm too stupid to get whatever's happening? Try me. Tell me, Dad."

"I don't think you're stupid."

She stepped into his space. "Then tell me. Tell. Me."

"They said they would hurt you!" he burst out. "They came back the next night and said they knew all about my family, that they'd seen you leaving the truck in the mornings. And that if I didn't go away, they'd do something to make us both go away."

She froze. "They... What?"

Dad sank into the chair, all of the anger seeming to drain out of him. "You heard me. I don't know what else to do. They're back almost every night now. So I thought... For a moment, I thought I should do what they said. Sell the truck."

Molten anger flowed through her. A minute ago, she'd been mad at being left out of the loop, but now she was on a new level of rage.

"Those assholes. This is racist, too. Am I right? They went after Anya because she's an immigrant, and you too."

Dad passed a hand over his face, looking even more tired. "Of course they're racists. And without any evidence, there's not much the police can do. Or so they told me. Right now, it's my word against theirs."

Sasha paced the length of the truck, hands clenching and unclenching. "This is a hate crime. We have to find those guys—"

"You're not going to find them." Dad straightened in his seat. "You're going to stay as far away from them as possible. This is exactly why I didn't want you to know."

"We have to fight back, though. We have to do something."

"What we have to do is take care of our own. Take care of what we have and keep it safe. With some hard work, we can—"

"Hard work doesn't fix everything. And it's leaving you exhausted."

He fixed her with his sternest look. "I know you think I'm too old to do this alone, but I've been alone for twenty years now. I'll be fine. Sasha, you will not take chances with yourself."

She stopped pacing. "That's why you didn't tell me. You think I'm going to go do something dumb."

Dad's gaze stayed steady on her. "I lost part of my family, and I'm not willing to lose any more."

Of course this would have triggered Dad's fears of losing her, like he'd lost Mom. But this was different. The injustice of it rose in her throat, threatening to choke her.

"I don't take chances with myself."

He snorted a laugh. "That's funny. You're making a joke."

"I don't. Dad, you know I'm not going to try to hunt these guys down by myself. Or at least, not without a good plan," she added.

"Promise me you won't do anything. You asked me to wait on the idea of selling the truck. Now I am asking you to not go off half-cocked and chase down dangerous criminals. I'm going to go back to the police station in the morning and try to file a report again."

"Sounds super promising." She couldn't keep the bitterness out of her tone.

"Some things take persistence. Not every situation requires rushing into action, like you seem to believe. My little tiger," he added with a half smile.

Some of the anger drained out of her. Anyone else who called her that would receive a punch, but Dad had always been proud of her fire. He'd supported it. If he wanted her to wait, she'd try to.

"Fine. I'll wait. And I did inherit my temper from someone, you know."

"No idea who." He patted her arm and turned to the kitchen, surveying the area with his hands on his hips.

"Your friend did okay. The dishes don't have spots. He can come back if he wants to."

"I'll let him know."

Dad huffed out a sigh and went to move the car. She sank into a chair and shut her eyes. Waiting was not what she wanted to do. But like so many times before, life had boxed her in and left her with too few choices. Between fighting and doing nothing, she'd always chosen to fight.

Because if she didn't have the fight, she was just a person who let things happen to her. And she'd never been that woman.

Chapter 8

C ameron opened the food truck door the next morning to a blast of onion fumes so strong, he took a step backward.

"Come on in," Sasha called. "It's onion day."

"I could tell," he muttered, climbing the steps to the truck. Everything inside the truck was a blur. He removed his glasses and swiped at his eyes.

"How are you seeing well enough to hold a knife right now, much less use it?" he asked as he approached her. "And why don't you have a food processor?"

Her hands flew over the cutting board in a sure, practiced motion. She spared him a glance over her shoulder.

"Dad says it doesn't taste the same, and they have to be hand-diced. Now, that's probably superstition on his part, but I don't argue with him about the recipe. And don't rub your eyes. That makes it worse."

Her tone was short, her posture tense as she chopped. She seemed less relaxed than yesterday, or maybe he was imagining things.

"Okay." He pulled out his pocket square and dabbed at his face.

Sasha stopped chopping. "Do you…carry a handkerchief in your pocket?"

"It's better for the environment and—" He cut himself off at the amused look she was giving him. "Never mind."

She shook her head. "I swear you were born in the wrong century."

If he'd been born a century ago, he wouldn't be tied to his laptop, a thought that had occurred to him more than once.

"So. Onions today."

"I thought we could get ahead on the prep. When I'm alone, I manage to take care of one day's work, but with the two of us working, we could get Dad set up for next week, too."

"Sounds like a plan." He rubbed his eyes with his sleeve, and she regarded him with a resigned expression.

"I can't put a knife in your hand if you can't see."

"I agree, it wouldn't be smart."

"Then you're peeling potatoes."

She set down her knife, went to the fridge, and pulled out two large bags of potatoes. She set up a cutting board, peeler, and a bowl of water on the opposite end of the counter from her onion operation.

She gestured at the board. "I assume you've peeled potatoes."

"Yeah, I can manage that."

She observed over his shoulder as he worked, then gave a nod of approval. "Put them in the water when they're done, so they don't turn brown."

"Got it."

She turned her back on him and went back to her chopping.

She was silent for a long time, not seeming to want to talk like she had yesterday. His first instinct had been right. Something was bothering her. Her movements with the knife were sure and practiced, but she was using too much force, like the vegetables had offended her personally. He had a strong sense it wouldn't be smart for him to say so.

To fill the space, he talked. Sometimes, problems could be approached in a roundabout way, and asking directly didn't seem like the right choice right now.

"So. I took a nap when I got home yesterday. I never take naps."

Her knife stopped for a second, hovering over the board. "I knew it. Manual labor plus excessive carbs works every time."

He shook his head, still not believing he'd done it. He'd gone home and sat on the couch, intending to get up in a minute. When he'd opened his eyes two hours later, he'd had a crick in his neck, and it was halfway dark outside.

"It must have done something to me. I don't sleep well."

"And did you feel better when you woke up?" she asked.

"I felt groggy. Forgot what day it was, or what I was supposed to be doing."

"Maybe that's a good thing for you. You should do it more often."

"Maybe." He paused to wipe his eyes again.

"Wait 'til we start frying these onions," she said with a tiny smile. "Then we're really cooking with gas."

He gave a dramatic groan, and a laugh burst out of her. He'd surprised that sound from her, and he wanted to do it again. Why it was so important to make her laugh, and also to figure out what was bothering her, was the bigger question.

For one thing, her face transformed when she smiled, leaving her face less guarded, more open. The first few times they'd met, he'd been overwhelmed by her hotness. It had taken all his concentration not to stare at her tattoos, at her curves in the tank tops she wore. Hot women were as unapproachable as the sun, and shouldn't be looked at directly.

But her genuine smile was far more dangerous. It lit her up from the inside, and made him imagine what it might be like to see it more often. Maybe even after this week was over.

Which was not the plan. He was doing her a favor after his colossal misstep at their first meeting. Nothing more than that would happen between them. She was a patient at the clinic, and even if she wasn't, she seemed on her guard, and under stress from the difficult times her family faced. And he had no time for dating anyway.

He shook himself out of it and made himself peel more potatoes, while she set a large frying pan on the stove and heated oil in the bottom.

"Onions are the main seasoning we use," she told him as she scraped the contents of her cutting board over the pan. "Well, onions and salt."

"Onions are high in vitamin C."

"See? They're good for you. And they taste good. But they make you work for it."

Steam billowed from the pan, and the air grew impossibly thicker with the scent.

"I'm taking a break." He set down his peeler and threw open the door to the truck, taking deep gulps of the fresh air. Her laughter followed him from inside.

Sasha was like an onion. She had a sharp bite and lots of layers. And maybe she was capable of sweetness, too.

A few minutes later, she joined him on the front steps of the truck. They stood side by side at the railing, looking out over the square.

"I turned the heat down to low," she said. "I'll go in and stir every few minutes, but this part takes a long time. Never trust anyone who says you can caramelize an onion in ten minutes. They've never cooked if they talk like that."

"Liars." He gave a sage nod, and the corner of her mouth went up.

This was the moment when he could ask more about what was bothering her. And something was up. She'd been quieter, more short in her responses today.

He slid a glance her way. "So, you want to tell me what happened?"

Her gaze sharpened. "What do you mean?"

"You were upset about something when I got here."

She cocked her head to the side, regarding him. "And you're too observant."

"Part of my job. Well, my future job, I hope."

"Right." She propped her elbows on the railing. "And I don't like talking to counselors."

"I'm not your counselor, but I could…" He cut himself off, shaking his head.

"Could what?"

"I was about to say, I could be your friend. But I'm not sure that's right, either."

She shook her head. "I just met you, and this is not a permanent arrangement, you helping out here." She gestured between him and the door of the truck.

"Of course I know that."

"So why do you care?"

"I'm not sure I get it, either." She stayed silent, forcing him to sort through the rest of his thoughts. "I think partly, I need a distraction from my work right now. And partly, I'm curious. But also..." He turned to face her. "Maybe there's something else I could do to help."

And also, I'm attracted to you, and I shouldn't be.

"I don't think you can help," she said. "Other than what you're already doing this week. Which, thank you for that. But I guess it wouldn't hurt to tell you what's going on, since I won't see you after this week. Look at me, opening up and everything."

"You don't have to."

"No, it's fine. I think, weirdly enough, I can trust you. I found out yesterday Dad has been lying to me about the vandalism. It's not random. They're targeting him after he helped Anya, one of the other food truck owners. Then they threatened to hurt me. Freaked him out enough that he thought about selling the truck."

Cameron stood up straighter, ice shooting down his spine. "Did he report it?"

"He did. But with no evidence, they told him they can't do much. He's going to try again today to file a report, not that it'll do any good. He made me promise to keep waiting and sit on my hands, which I'm pretty bad at."

"What about security cameras? They're a lot less expensive than they used to be."

"He bought some, but they destroyed them. More than once. We can't keep buying new cameras every few days. That adds up."

"There has to be something else we can do." His brain whirred to life. There was more than one way to get documentation of what was happening.

She turned to face him, her expression curious. "Careful. You said 'we.'"

"This is…not right. That your dad has to be scared for your safety, and no one's doing anything to stop it."

"It isn't right." She squared her shoulders, her tone taking on a hard edge. "It's also not right that I went to court on assault charges and destruction of property, and the bad guy got away. The world is pretty unfair, all in all. I'm going to stir the onions."

She turned and disappeared inside the truck door. He'd hit a nerve, and he couldn't blame her. Her situation *was* unfair.

When she came back out a few minutes later, he'd thought of another question.

"Can I ask you something? About the night you got into the fight?"

"Sure, why not?" She sounded resigned now, some of the anger from a few minutes ago gone.

"That night… You said you put a man through a glass window?"

The corner of her mouth turned up. "Not all the way through it. Just sort of…shattered the glass with his torso. It was very satisfying. Until he got away."

He cleared his throat, his stomach flip-flopping at the thought of her facing down some thug by herself.

"Were you injured? Did he hurt you?"

She held up her index finger. "One punch. He got one punch in. My jaw was swollen, but other than that, I was fine."

"So wasn't that evidence he'd attacked you? That he was the perpetrator, and you acted in self-defense?"

"Yeah, my public defense argued that angle. But first of all, we had no evidence of the vandalism they'd been doing for weeks ahead of that night. And also…I might not have explained it all that well, either. So it looked like a random street fight. And then I'd damaged private property to the tune of thousands of dollars. So I got a sentence. And he got to disappear."

"Huh." The sliver of unease from a moment ago uncoiled in his gut, taking up more space.

She frowned over at him. "Does it bother you to hear that?"

"Not for the reasons you think." He met her gaze, which had gone all guarded again.

"I bet you've never been in a fight in your life."

"I don't like violence, it's true. My brother got into some bad situations as a teenager, and my parents—well, mostly my mom—had to clean up after him a lot. I saw my share of fights growing up."

"So you had to be the good son, because your brother was the trouble-maker."

That was far too close to the truth. He'd spent countless nights cooking dinner for Mom, so she could rest after a draining day of visiting Robbie in rehab or attending school meetings to discuss his latest detention.

"I just prefer to think things through, instead of rushing into a fight."

She snorted a laugh. "I've been told to do the same thing recently. So what would you do if someone attacked you? Let them?"

"Of course I'd defend myself. Robbie taught me to fight by jumping me at every opportunity when we were kids. But to answer your question, I'd try to avoid getting myself into the situation in the first place. Think of another way out of it."

Her expression hardened. "Sometimes conflict is unavoidable."

"Yeah. I get that. You were in an impossible situation. You fought back. And I realized something else while you were talking earlier."

"What's that?"

"I don't think you have an anger management problem. Not like Robbie had a drug problem. He went after trouble at every chance he got. You were defending yourself."

She let out a long breath. "Yeah. I was. But also, it was fun, hitting that guy."

He felt a smile threaten the corner of his mouth. "That's where you and I are different."

"Hold onto that thought. Got to stir onions."

She disappeared again, and when she came back, the sweet scent of caramelized onions blasted out the door.

"It's getting better, right?" she asked.

"Yeah." He cleared his throat. "Feels like I won't die if I go in there now."

"Good. Come back inside. It's cold out."

He followed her back into the truck, where he found her scraping the browned onions into a stainless steel mixing bowl.

"So it's your professional opinion that I don't have anger issues."

"I'm not diagnosing you. But I do think the system treated you like crap, and you had a right to be mad."

She paused scraping for a moment, shook her head, and then continued the motion.

"What?" he asked, examining her face.

"You keep surprising me. I didn't expect you, of all people, to get that."

"Because I'm a counselor? I think anyone could get that

about you."

She shook her head. "Nope. My whole life, people treated me like I was less than them, because we were poor, and immigrants, and my parents didn't speak a lot of English at first. It always made me so mad. I know I acted out as a kid. And of course now, they treat me like a violent criminal."

"Well, you're not. That's not how I see you."

"Thank you." She set down the heavy skillet with a thunk, her gaze steady on his. Her eyes were softer than he'd ever seen them, shining blue and brown.

He was having trouble getting in a breath, looking at her. He'd almost taken a step toward her before he realized it and stopped himself. What had he been about to do? Hug her?

She'd probably punch him before she'd hug him. But she didn't look like she wanted to punch him. He shifted his eyes away first.

She cleared her throat. "So. One of the things that helps me when I feel like the world is unfair is helping other people learn to fight. When I teach self-defense to women, it helps me feel like I'm not doing nothing. Like my anger has a purpose."

"That's a great way to look at it."

"Would you want to see my gym?" she said in a rush. "It'd have to be after hours, because of the no-men rule. But I'd like to show it to you."

"I'd like to see it."

"Really?" She seemed almost unsure, which made no sense.

But now she'd suggested it, he wanted to see her there, in her element. That way, in the future, when they were no longer in contact, he could picture her there. Guiding a class or teaching lessons, helping others learn to fight like she did.

And he'd get to see her again, which was somehow the most

85

important thing to come out of this conversation. They had three mornings left in his volunteer arrangement. Then it would be over, and he'd be back at school, back to the endless gray march of data reports.

"Really," he told her.

"Good. Then I'll text you the address."

He saw a hint of a smile before she turned to take the skillet to the dish sink. He grabbed his peeler and went back to the potatoes.

Chapter 9

Sasha checked her watch as she waited in the center of the workout floor, then flicked her gaze out the windows. She'd asked Cameron to come here at 9:00, after the place emptied out following evening classes.

Maybe it had been a bad impulse to invite him here. To show him a part of her life other men hadn't been allowed to see. Their conversations over the last few days must have tricked her brain into thinking she could trust him.

The feeling persisted all afternoon, though. That she wanted to see him again. And she might even be a tiny bit disappointed when this week was over.

He was more attractive than her initial estimate of him. She'd thought he was cute in a nerdy way, but there was more to him than that. Something in the way his serious hazel eyes focused on her from behind his glasses when he listened. The way his curls always looked messy, as if he'd run his hands through them.

He was the kind of guy she might look past in a crowd. But

having his attention focused on her was something else. It was a powerful feeling, being listened to. Maybe the most attractive thing a man had ever done with her.

In the past, she'd been with guys who wanted fun and no commitments, which had worked for both of them. She doubted Cameron was that kind of guy, though. He was too cautious, too thoughtful for the one-night stands she preferred.

And maybe a tiny part of her wanted to test if this feeling was real, find out how he'd respond to an advance. But it was better to push down that impulse. For once in her life, she'd restrain her tendency to act first and ask questions later.

She could be restrained when necessary. It just wasn't as much fun.

His tall, rangy form approached the glass door, and she hurried to open it for him. The bell on the door jingled as she held it open for him, and he jogged up the steps to the door, a leather bag under his arm.

He had jeans on again tonight, and another of the Henley shirts he liked, with the sleeves pushed up to the elbows. He looked more relaxed than he had the last couple of days, better rested.

"You made it," she told him.

"I did. Thanks for asking me."

She gestured him inside and locked the door behind him.

"So, did you take another nap this afternoon?"

He shook his head ruefully. "I can't believe it, but I did. Two afternoons in a row. I got home from the food truck and fell asleep on the couch again."

"I told you, physical labor plus carbs."

"Yeah, you did. But I can't do this every day. I have schoolwork. My spring break is over in a few days." He rubbed a hand over the back of his neck. "Besides, I woke up groggy again."

"Your body's catching up. Groggy's better than exhausted."

He raised a brow at her. "Debatable. I'm less functional this way."

She folded her arms across her chest. "You seem to care more about being functional than feeling good."

His brows went down, as if she'd said the most obvious thing in the world. "Of course I do. Anyway, thanks for inviting me here."

"You should feel lucky. Most men never see the inside of this place. You want a quick tour?"

"Yeah, show me."

She led him into the main area of the gym, where padded mats stretched wall to wall.

"So this open area is where we do big classes. Most of the martial arts groups need more space. We have a weight room and a workout room in the back. And three individual rooms for private lessons."

She led him down the tiled hallway to the weight room. As he followed her, he looked around, seeming to take it all in, and she tried to picture it through his eyes. The building was older and needed new signage and a coat of paint on the outside. To her, that made the space even better, more lived-in.

"This is the gym. Some women come here to work out, some to take classes."

The vinyl gym mats were clean but worn, the weight lifting equipment well used. Two treadmills and two elliptical machines stood in the back corner.

"It seems cozy. I bet people like it better than the bigger gyms."

"They do. Fewer people staring at you." She motioned for him to follow her to the next doorway.

"This is the workout room. And then there's the locker room and the smaller rooms down the hall."

They stood in the doorway of the workout room, where four punching bags hung from the ceiling, one in each corner.

"Do you use this room for classes, too?" he asked.

"Sometimes for kickboxing lessons. Or for a small self-defense class, too."

She put her hands on her hips, suddenly self-conscious. "And that's about it."

Why had she asked him here? It was strange seeing a man in the building at all. He couldn't be impressed with the old building and small rooms. He couldn't know everything it meant to her, even if the mats and props were worn. The smell of sweat and disinfectant felt as much like home to her as the onion smell of the food truck.

But as usual, Cameron didn't seem to judge.

"Do you work out here?" he asked, still looking around the space.

"Yeah. I get here early most days so I can do my own workout before I start teaching."

"It must be nice. To get to do something where you shut off your brain for a while."

He sounded almost wistful. This man never shut off his brain at all.

"Dad enrolled me in karate classes when I was five. I had a lot of energy, and I was pretty mad most of the time. He figured I could use some training up."

He tilted his head to the side. "You mentioned people treating you...not as an equal."

"Yeah, I got bullied a lot in school. It started early, but it never went away. I guess Dad thought I should at least be able to defend myself."

"He had a good idea." He drew in a breath. "People really gave you a hard time, though? I can't picture it, somehow. With how you are now."

"Oh, yeah. Kids don't like someone who's different. I was poor, and I wasn't thin, for starters. And I couldn't read very well. Dyslexia."

His brows went down. "I'm sorry they teased you."

"Well, after a while, they learned not to," she said lightly. "But then I got in trouble with the school administrators for fighting. One time, I got called into the assistant principal's office after a fight. He told me they wanted to hear all the sides of the story. And like an idiot, I believed him and told him everything. Only to get suspended for a week for threatening another student's safety."

"But that's not what you did." He said it with so much certainty, his eyes steady on her.

"How do you know?"

"I just know you wouldn't threaten someone. Not unless they were hurting you."

She shifted her eyes to the floor, suddenly uncomfortable with the eye contact. "Well, you're right. Not that it helped me in that situation. After that, I shut up and didn't bother trying to explain myself to administrators."

"Let me guess. The same thing happened in your police interview. You didn't bother to explain the whole story, because you didn't think they'd listen."

"Yep. That's about it."

"What do you think would happen if you did tell them everything? I know it's your word against theirs, but what if you let them know the full truth? Everything you experienced?"

"I don't know." She folded her arms across her chest. "It's too late now, anyway."

Cameron studied her for a long minute before he spoke again.

"Would you show me? Some of your martial arts? I mean, only if you want to."

"You want what? A skills demonstration?"

His eyes held hers, an expression she'd never seen in them flickering under the surface.

"I want to see how you beat that guy up. I've tried to picture it, but I can't. I think if you showed me… I don't know. Maybe it's a bad idea."

"I'll do it," she told him.

She never showed off, never performed, and especially not for a man. Her fighting was for herself and for self-defense. But this wasn't showing off. She wanted him to see what she did best, so he'd understand what happened that night.

Sharing this part of herself with another person should have terrified her, but excitement thrummed through her veins.

"Stand over there," she told him.

She pointed him to a corner and stripped off her sweatshirt. Underneath, she wore a sports bra and track pants, the clothing she usually worked out in.

His eyes skimmed over her torso, then darted away. Let him look, though. Here, she was in her element, at home.

She set the punching bag swinging, simulating a man ducking and weaving in front of her. Jumping from side to side, she talked him through the basics.

"Mostly, it's about anticipating the other guy's movement.

They lunge, you step back. They fall back, you move in. It's a dance."

She landed a couple of punch combos and danced back from the answering swing of the bag. Cameron stood silent in the corner.

"You look for an opening, a weak spot. If you have enough space, you move back and land a kick."

She spun into a high kick, and the bag lurched backward with a satisfying thwack. She repeated the move, starting to enjoy herself. She felt Cameron's gaze, his intent watching. Something she never thought she'd enjoy, but she felt her skin heat further under his perusal.

She spun into a series of kickboxing moves, and they felt good. Her limbs flowed through the familiar series of motions and her body calmed, her mind cleared.

This was why she fought. Not out of aggression, but because the fight and the anger were their own kind of peace, their own clarity. All the days she'd hit the gym in high school, frustrated because she couldn't keep up with the class reading in Language Arts, or because someone told her that her hair smelled like onions, she'd been comforted by this. This pure exertion.

This was her, telling her truth.

"So that night." She swung a series of fast punches at the bag because she could. A light sheen of sweat covered her torso. "This guy was big, but slow. Clumsy. He kept lunging at me, but he was easy to avoid. I was a lot faster, and I had the element of surprise. He didn't know I could fight. So I used his size against him."

She ducked and lunged at the bag, hitting it with her shoulder and using the force of her legs to propel it forward a couple of feet. She jumped out of the way to avoid its wide arc on the way back down.

"Just like that. Man through a window."

She paused, hands on her hips, her chest going up and down with exertion. The punching bag swung in front of her, decreasing its arc with each pass.

Cameron stayed silent in the corner. After a moment, she met his eyes. He'd been leaning against the wall, and he stepped away from it, walking toward her, his expression unreadable. But there was something underneath. Something more than admiration and closer to desire.

"That was...really amazing. Thank you for showing me."

"Thank you for asking to see it."

"I can see why you love it. It suits you."

She cocked her head to the side. "Don't you have something you love, too? A hobby? Sport?"

He shook his head. "Maybe once, in the past. But not like that. Not so...all-consuming."

His chest expanded on an inhale.

"I already knew I wanted to help you more, even before I came here tonight," he said slowly. "But now... Now I know it's the right choice. We need to catch those guys. You defended yourself, but that doesn't mean you should have to do it again."

He stood a few steps away from her, carefully not looking at her chest. Most men couldn't keep their eyes above her neck, but he seemed to be avoiding looking down at all costs.

"What do you mean, help me more?" she asked.

"I did something uncharacteristic, for me. Something I never would have done in the past. But I guess I've been doing all kinds of unusual things since I met you."

"I don't understand."

94

He held up the leather bag he'd brought, shaking it.

"I took a camera from our research lab. I'm going to say 'borrowed,' because it sounds better than 'stole.' We use them for sleep studies. It'll get better quality footage than a standard security cam, because it's designed to work in low light. And it's good for filming from longer distances."

Her brain raced to catch up. "You're lending us a camera? But that's expensive. They'll—"

He shook his head. "They won't have a chance to destroy it, because we're not going to put it in your dad's truck. We're going to put it in his friend's truck, across the street."

"That...could actually work." A rush of hope filled her chest, light and warm. "If the camera is as good as you said."

"It is. Damn things cost enough," he added.

"Thank you." On impulse, she flung her arms around his waist, heard his sharp intake of breath. His body was lean and strong against hers. Full of his own kind of strength. A thoughtful strength. The sort of strength that didn't prove itself by punching.

He didn't hug her back right away, remaining frozen in her arms for a beat.

"Cameron. This is called a hug. Human beings like to do this sometimes."

He huffed out a laugh, and his arms went around her, looping around her waist and giving her a soft squeeze.

She stepped away from him after a moment and looked up at his face.

"Sorry if that was too forward. I should have asked."

His eyes darkened. "It's not that. It's... I haven't been hugged in a long time. No. It's more than that." He shoved a hand through his curls. "I'm attracted to you, and I don't know what

95

to do with myself."

"Are you." She took a step closer again, back into his space, unable to stop herself from teasing him.

The man was nothing if not honest, and when you were honest about your weak points, someone was bound to take advantage.

He took a shuddering inhale. "Yep. That's what this is. It's been a while for me on that, too."

"Don't you ever date?"

"I had a girlfriend in college. But not since I've been in grad school."

He still wouldn't look anywhere but at her face, but standing this close to him, she could feel the tension radiating off him, from the still way he held himself to the fists clenching at his sides.

"And you've been in grad school for how long?"

"Seven years in May. Three on my Master's and four on my PhD."

She took one tiny step closer, so their chests almost touched. "Cameron. Are you telling me you haven't had sex in seven years?"

A dull red crept up his face. "Other things were more important."

"Hmm." She lifted a hand and almost laid it on his chest, which was rising and falling more rapidly than it had been a moment ago.

At the last minute, she pulled her hand away, because she shouldn't play with him like this. The man had stolen expensive lab equipment for her, so she should return the favor by not teasing him.

Or maybe she'd be doing him a favor by following this

attraction and seeing where it went.

She stepped away from him, crossed the room, and retrieved her sweatshirt from where she'd dropped it on the mat. She slid it over her head and turned to him.

"So. No food, no sleep, and no sex for seven years."

"You make it sound like I'm an android."

"Sometimes I wonder if you are. Can we go set the camera up tonight? Right now?"

Cameron blinked at the subject change, but to his credit, he went with it.

"Sure. We can go now."

Chapter 10

The downtown parking lot was dark and almost empty when Cameron arrived. A minute later, Sasha's red sedan zipped into the spot next to his, and for no good reason, his heart rate accelerated. Again.

That hug. The look on her face when he'd told her about the camera he'd stolen—borrowed—from the lab for her. He'd broken the rules for this woman, and that meant one of two things. He'd either reached a level of burnout where he had no grip on reality at all anymore. Or he was developing feelings for Sasha.

It was probably the former. For it to be the latter, he'd have to believe that two days working together in a food truck and one incredibly hot martial arts demonstration were enough to get under his skin. He'd been so focused on school the past few years, and that meant pushing the possibility of dating and relationships out of his mind. He had no time or energy to devote to feelings.

Apparently, letting himself take time off work equaled opening himself up to the possibility of messy, time-consuming emotions. But that couldn't be what this was. This was a sprout of a feeling, a tendril of attraction, which he could cut off when it was time to say goodbye next week.

A person could live a very fulfilling life and stay single. And tonight wasn't a date, either.

But for a minute, when he'd let himself wrap his arms around Sasha and felt the press of her soft warmth against him, a thread of tension had loosened in his chest. As if he'd been stitched together too tightly, and someone had eased the strain. But he wouldn't be taking that feeling further. Even if the thought was more compelling than school, or work, or anything else for a long time.

And now they were getting out of their cars, smiling at each other like school kids about to run away from the teacher on a field trip as they snuck behind the row of food trucks.

Sasha gestured for him to follow her. "Anya's truck's this way."

She kept her voice pitched low, not that there was anyone around to hear. "If she hasn't left for the night, we can ask her about putting the camera in her side window, facing our truck."

"That's what I thought, too. There's a clear view across the square, depending on the angle."

Sounds carried in the hush of the quiet street, and he followed her at a closer distance than he might have in daylight, holding his bag to his chest.

There was a real possibility the vandals who'd graffitied her truck would come back tonight. Maybe they were here now, waiting until the last few vendors left their trucks.

When they got to the momo truck, Sasha stopped, putting

her hands on her hips.

"She's already gone," she said. "I should've known she might close up early on a weeknight. She does that sometimes."

"We can try again tomorrow."

Before the words had left his mouth, Sasha had taken off at a fast walk around the side of the truck. He followed on her heels.

"What are you doing?" he whispered.

She'd dropped to her knees at the side of the truck and stuck her hand under the bumper, feeling around. A minute later, she pulled out a small box.

"Spare key," she said, holding it up.

"First of all—"

"I know, I know. It's not safe to leave a spare key right outside your vehicle. Dad's told her a hundred times. She does it anyway because she forgets and locks her keys inside all the time."

"Okay. And second, I'm sure she doesn't want you in there while she's gone."

She grinned up at him, her teeth flashing white in the dim light of the street lamp.

"She'll be okay with it. We'll come back tomorrow and explain what we did. She'd be on board if she was here right now."

Cameron drew in a deep breath. "If you say so."

"I do say so."

She had the truck door open a moment later, and he followed her inside. She pulled the door closed behind them. The lingering smell of curry filled the tiny space, and he froze at the entrance.

"Second thoughts?" she asked, turning to face him.

"I just… I don't know what I'm doing here."

Stealing lab equipment, breaking and entering, and leaving the stolen equipment in a stranger's truck were all things that normal Cameron would never do. But normal Cameron seemed to have taken a vacation this week—for once in his life.

He shook his head. "Never mind. Let's do it."

She gave a sharp nod. "Okay. This side window has the clearest view of Dad's truck. We should put it here, and angle it so it points that way."

He stepped past her and examined the window, which was covered by plastic blinds.

"We can hide the camera behind the blinds and fit the lens through one of the slats. From the outside, I don't think they'll see it."

"Perfect. Because if they saw it, they'd break the window." She frowned, looking concerned for the first time.

"They won't," he reassured her. "The lens is small, and from far away, it'll be invisible. You'd have to know to look for it."

He sat on the bench seat under the window, and Sasha joined him. He extracted the camera from his bag, checked the memory card he'd inserted one more time, and pressed the power button. When the blinking red light came on, indicating it was recording, he placed it on the windowsill and adjusted the lens until it fit between the blinds.

"Does this angle look right?" he asked.

Sasha reached across him and moved the camera a few degrees to the left. "That should capture the action around our truck. It's recording now?"

"Yep. It has a long battery life, but we can come back and recharge it every couple of days. We can check the memory card then, or if something happens sooner, we'll know we caught footage of it."

"I can't believe it's that easy." She shook her head. "Just like that, we're going to have evidence."

The corner of his mouth turned up. "Scientific researchers are good at getting evidence. It's one of our skills. We'll get this footage."

"That's a very good skill to have." She stared at him for a beat, then stood and brushed a hand down her sweatshirt. "I guess that's it, then. We should probably get out of here and lock up."

Outside the truck, she locked the door and stowed the spare key in its spot. She turned to face him, leaning against the side of the truck. The cool night air stirred around them, bringing with it the scent of the blooming lilac bushes along the sides of the square.

"Thank you again," she said. "I don't think anyone's offered to help us like this before. It means a lot. To hear you say 'we,' like we're a team or something."

Her expression was so sincere, so far from the guarded version of her he'd met at first. Her eyes shone up at him in the dim light, a deep liquid brown swirled with blue, like a globe. The whole world was in her eyes, a world far more vivid and alive than the dull version he'd been existing in.

Maybe that was why words came out of his mouth that normal Cameron would never say, ever, under any circumstances.

"I think we're a good team," he told her.

Her brows went up. "Are we?"

"We're friends, at least," he backtracked. "Or we could be. If you wanted. And friends help each other out with what they need."

"This is… You have to understand, this is all new to me. I'm not sure I can say I've been friends with a man before."

"No?"

She shook her head. "Nope. Mostly, I use men for sex."

He choked on his next indrawn breath and let out a ragged cough. "That's honest, at least."

She took a step closer to him, then another, until she was right in his space. "And what about what you need? You said friends help each other with what they need."

"I…" His brain had suddenly filled with white static, and no other words came to him.

"You said you're attracted to me, and you don't know what to do about it."

His heart beat faster than seemed advisable for his health. She took one last step closer, her chest almost brushing his now. His brain continued its odd silence as she reached out, grabbed his hand, and gave it a tug.

"C'mon."

She laced her fingers between his and pulled him a few steps away from the truck, and he followed, helpless. She led him into an alcove between the storefronts lining the square. He ducked under the awning and faced her, less sure of what was happening than ever before in his life.

In the shadowy space, she stepped close to him, pressed herself against his front. He sucked in a sharp breath.

"Is this okay?"

He took a shuddering inhale. "Yeah." Whatever she wanted, the answer would be yes.

"Okay if I kiss you, too?"

"Yes." He needed that, more than his next meal, more than air.

Carefully, she reached up and took off his glasses. She folded them, handed them to him, and he slid them into his breast pocket.

She leaned in, placed her hand on the side of his jaw, and a full-body shiver went through him. She stroked the side of his face, like he was a nervous horse about to bolt, and maybe he was. Though not away from her. To her.

She had to stand on her tiptoes to ease her mouth close to his. She was being gentle, probably trying to take it easy on him, since his chest was already pumping up and down like he'd run a mile.

And then her mouth touched his, and his body exploded into feeling. His eyes fell shut, colored sparks dancing behind them, and he could only experience the sensation of her lips, their softness, the way they pressed against his. She moved her mouth against his slowly, then with increasing purpose. Pushing to get inside.

He opened to her, and was even further lost when she pressed into his mouth, stroking her tongue against his. He bent his head to take more, to feel more of her.

Her hand came up to the back of his neck, and another shudder went through him. His body was as restless and on edge as he could ever remember, the explosion of sensations almost too much for his brain to process.

This was not like kissing had been in the past. Kissing had always been nice, a pleasant way to feel close to another person. To express affection. Not like someone had lit a fire inside his chest, and he'd die if he didn't get closer to the source of the heat.

His arm went around her waist and yanked her closer. He was not being as gentle as she'd been a moment ago. He felt greedy, drunk on her, and he wanted more. This wasn't like him, but he couldn't seem to stop himself from gripping her hips and holding her tight against him.

She groaned at the action, and the kiss detonated. No more gentle exploration, but more of a devouring. He wanted to swallow her down in a few quick bites.

Her hands slid into his hair, pulling his face to her as she pushed her weight forward into him. The momentum made him take a step backward, and his torso hit the brick wall behind him.

With her body pressed hard against him, his erection pushed against her middle, and that was almost too much for his overloaded senses. He ripped his mouth from hers and sucked in a breath, suddenly aware he was a hair's breadth away from coming. From a kiss.

And they were outside, in the open. In a square where dangerous criminals were looking for her.

His brain came back online with a shocking snap. This wasn't the place to lose control, not when she could be in danger. And not when, after this week, they'd never see one another again.

He stared at her, breath sawing in and out, inches between their faces.

She looked stunned. And also turned on, her pupils blown and mouth wet. His body screamed for him to keep going, but that would be the wrong thing to pay attention to. He'd always been good at ignoring his body, and he could do it again now.

"Well. That was fun. And unexpected." She laid a palm on his chest and gave him a crooked smile. She hadn't stepped away from him yet, and the feel of her breasts pressed against his chest was threatening to make him lose track of the reasons why this wasn't a good idea.

"It was…" He cleared his throat. "Yeah, it was fun. But maybe we should stop? It's not safe out here."

She glanced around, as if remembering where she was. "No one's around."

"Not now. But they could be."

She turned her amazing, hypnotic eyes back on him. "So what happens next? We go someplace? We do it again tomorrow?"

He straightened from the wall, took a careful step away from her. His body instantly cold from the loss of contact.

"I thought we were trying for friends." He tried to keep his tone light, neutral.

This was the right choice. The one that made sense. He didn't have time or space for dating, and she didn't date at all. She was fighting dangerous criminals and he was drowning in schoolwork.

"I get it." She shook her head with a half-smile. "No harm done."

She genuinely didn't sound upset about it. She'd said she did casual hookups with men, so maybe that kiss had been no big deal to her. The thought didn't comfort him.

Still, he knew her emotions from observing her over the past few days. Under the casual front, there'd been a flicker of feeling on her face just now. There one second and gone the next.

"You've got a lot going on, and so do I," he said. "Maybe it's better if we leave it at just friends."

No words had ever sounded lamer.

She held up her hand. "I get it. You're not into doing more. It was just for fun, anyway."

Unease slithered through his gut. A moment ago, everything had felt right. And now they were two magnets facing the wrong way, pushing each other apart.

But the moment was gone, and they were back to how they'd been before. He stepped away from the wall and caught her looking at him with an amused expression.

"What?" he asked.

"You've got flowers in your hair."

She reached up and brushed a few petals from his head, her fingers skimming the curls. A glance over his shoulder confirmed he'd been halfway against the wall, halfway in a lilac bush.

"There. Got them." She glanced around the square, clearly getting ready to go, and he fought the urge to pull her closer again.

"Guess I'll head home, then," she said.

He cleared his throat. "Tomorrow morning, I can come with you to Anya's. We can show her the camera."

"Sounds good. We can go first thing, so she doesn't freak out when she sees it."

"Yeah. Right."

"Well. See you tomorrow, then."

They walked to the parking lot in silence. When they got to their cars, she gave him a casual wave over the hood before sliding behind the driver's seat and taking off. He sat behind the steering wheel for a long time before starting the ignition and heading home.

Chapter 11

C ameron's shoes clicked on the tile as he made his way down the hallway to Dr. Gold's office for their update meeting. When he'd set up the time, he'd imagined that by halfway through his spring break, he'd have made some solid progress on the study. But between three days of working in the food truck in the morning and taking mysterious naps in the afternoons, he hadn't made much headway on redoing the data analyses for the study.

And his habit of caring about the quality of his work seemed to have died for the time being. Small details like his PhD faded into the background in the face of what had happened last night.

The kiss replayed on a loop in his head, every detail engraved on his memory.

It wasn't just that it had been a good kiss. A mind-numbingly amazing kiss. It was his own response to it that he couldn't pin down, couldn't define. His skin had been too tight for his body, from the moment she grabbed his hand until the moment she walked away from him.

He'd felt an uncomfortable ache under his breastbone as she drove away. He'd never had trouble separating from his emotions, but that didn't mean he couldn't recognize them. He was getting attached to her. He liked her, and that was not something he should pursue right now.

Dating his girlfriend in college had been fun, but it hadn't touched the flow of his work. When it had been time to get more serious about grad school, his relationship had fallen away, leaving no room for anything except working toward his goals. They'd had fun, but it hadn't hurt much when they'd broken up.

Sasha was already different, his attraction to her stronger and more volatile. A powder keg threatening to blow. Three days of spending time with her, and he couldn't focus on anything else, couldn't think straight. And that was bad, because he still had this study to complete, his dissertation to finish writing, and he'd wasted half of spring break already.

This morning, when he'd shown up to volunteer, she'd been all business, brisk and cheerful and holding him at a distance. Which was fine.

They'd kissed, but now they were back to normal. They were friends. They'd gone to Anya's truck and showed her the camera, and the older woman had agreed it was a good idea. Then they'd made bread dough together and peeled potatoes and done the dishes.

All of which was completely fine and normal. Now he could return to his normal life and buckle down to finish his study.

He raised a hand to knock on Dr. Gold's door, squeezing his laptop in his fist. He'd make up something, buy some extra time, and try to hide how little work he'd gotten done in the last two weeks.

Gold called for him to come in, and he opened the door to find his advisor standing at the window, arms folded across his chest. He arched a brow at Cameron, an infuriatingly superior expression.

"You're late."

"Only a few minutes." Cameron took his usual seat in the chair across from Gold's desk. The other man remained standing, looking down at him a moment longer before finally taking a seat at the desk.

"I want to hear about your progress. But before that, we have some additional information to go over."

"Okay." The additional information could have been sent in an email, but whatever it was, he'd work with it.

Cameron cleared his throat. "I've started revising to account for the missing segments of data—"

"You can stop that." Gold cut him off with a slashing gesture of his hand. "What we've got in front of us now is a bit more complex."

Cameron straightened in his chair. "What do you mean?"

"I found two more areas where the data wasn't filtered correctly. You'll have to start over again."

"That's not possible."

Gold cocked his head to the side. "I assure you, it is."

"There has to be a mistake. You—" He cut himself off before he blamed his supervisor, who was supposed to check the data before handing it off to him.

"No, this was all you." His advisor spun his laptop around, pointing to a spreadsheet of one of their research stages he'd pulled up on the screen. "After I transferred the data to you, you were supposed to filter out this subset of participants before you did your analyses."

Cameron pulled the laptop closer and pushed his glasses up his nose. A quick scan of the highlighted columns confirmed Gold was right. He froze, his brain trying to process the new information.

He'd assumed the data errors had come from Gold not doing his part. But it had been his own fault. He'd prided himself on never making mistakes, on the perfect precision of his study. But his brain must have failed him, because the error was right in front of him.

He sucked in a breath. "That was me. I'm sorry."

"Don't be sorry. Put in the work to fix it."

It would be a mountain of work. More work than one person could get done before May.

He swallowed. "Do we have anyone available to assist? One of the first-year students, maybe?"

"Everyone's booked up. Besides, you're the one who knows this study inside and out. This is your mistake, and you'll need to correct it."

He drew in deep breaths. Told himself the man didn't mean to sound smug, but it just came out that way.

"But if you can't manage it, we can delay submitting your dissertation, of course," Gold added. "Let me know if you need an extension."

"That won't be necessary." Cameron kept his voice steady and calm.

Inside, his gut churned with an unfamiliar feeling. It was... anger? Anger at himself, for fucking things up. Because this mess *was* his fault. His level of burnout had made him sloppy, leading to a massive mistake he might not be able to fix in time.

But the anger wasn't only directed at himself. It was for his insufferable supervisor. For the whole ridiculous system that put so much pressure on grad students.

No one could survive this process and come out of it normal and healthy. It wasn't just a him problem.

He stood, the movement jerky and uncoordinated. "I'll get to work on that."

"Good. Let me know if you have any questions."

Dr. Gold turned to his laptop and started typing. No doubt emailing other hapless grad students and heaping extra work on them.

He shut the man's office door with a quiet click. Now was the part where he was supposed to go home and panic-work all afternoon on the study. Pull an all-nighter, for however many nights it took, because sleep was less important than the ultimate goal of graduation.

His degree was on the line, and so was the potential of his future dream job at The Well Space. Spring break was half over. Then he'd be back to work full time, back to school. Now was his opportunity to cram in as much work as possible.

Instead, he found himself driving in the opposite direction from his apartment.

He used to care about things outside of work. He'd had interests that didn't involve data and research. But he'd let those things fall by the wayside, assuming school always had to come first.

Don't you have something you love?

Sasha's voice, her fierce determination as she whaled on the punching bag, had sparked something in him, and he hadn't been able to put a finger on what it was until now. She was passionate about something. She'd found the thing she loved.

And he'd been missing that.

He used to feel that way about psychology, until grad school had ground out the joy from it. Maybe he'd never find that feeling again in his chosen profession. But he'd felt it for other things, too, a long time ago.

He pulled into a parking space in front of what used to be his most common college hangout. A sense of lightness eased his chest as he pulled open the glass door of Heads or Tales Used and Rare Books, and the familiar smell of old paper greeted his nose.

The old man at the front desk, with his square jaw, white mustache, and sweater vest, squinted across at him.

"Is that Cameron? My eyes must be lying to me, though, because I was sure he moved away. He'd never stay away for this long if he still lived in town."

Cameron cleared his throat. "No, it's me. I got busy with school, but I missed this place." He hadn't realized how much until this moment. "It's good to see you, Luka."

"And you as well, my friend. Now, wait 'til you see what's come in since you were here last."

With the familiarity of an old friendship, Luka spoke to him as if they'd seen each other last week, rather than four years ago. It was like no time had passed, watching the older man ease himself out of his chair and beckon Cameron to follow him upstairs.

The downstairs level of the store sold used books, but upstairs carried rare editions, antiques, and collectors' items. The shop specialized in vintage sci-fi titles, and Luka had a nose for locating copies of the books his patrons were trying to find.

He followed the older man up the wooden staircase, an

unfamiliar feeling of anticipation lightening his steps. Which exploded into full-on excitement when the man pushed a cardboard box of vintage Star Trek comics across the counter at him.

"Oh my God."

Luka's smile was indulgent. "You shouldn't have stayed away so long."

"I…should not have. Can I…" He reached for the box.

"Of course. Look at as many as you want. You can remove them from the plastic if you want. It's a myth that people's fingers damage old books."

"Thank you so much."

"Of course. Have a seat over there, if you like."

Cameron took the box over to the armchair in the corner and sat with it balanced on his knees. He looked at it for a long moment before picking up the first comic in the stack.

It was ridiculous that he wanted to smell the books, run his hand over the covers. Even more ridiculous that he wanted to show them to Sasha. To tell her yes, he had things he cared about outside of work. Things that lit him up and brought him joy, even when he'd forgotten what it felt like.

She'd reconnected him to it, and as unlikely as their friendship was, it had brought him back to this. Tomorrow, he'd show her the comics he'd bought. He had a feeling he was about to buy a lot of them.

He sat in the armchair for the rest of the afternoon, sunlight streaming in the window and catching the dust motes as they floated around his head. He went home right before dinner, lighter in the wallet and with a dozen new titles to add to his collection.

At home, he pulled out the plastic storage boxes containing

his comic collection from the spare bedroom closet where he'd shoved them at some point, convinced he'd outgrown that part of his life. By 9:00 p.m., the entire room was covered in comics. He'd reread dozens of favorites, and he needed a new organization system. Maybe even a display case.

Food was also important—he'd need to eat dinner. And maybe, at some point, he should look at his homework. Sleep would be a long time coming, though, and not because of stress.

On impulse, he pulled out his phone to text Sasha. Because friends shared things they were excited about with one another, and he hadn't had anyone to share things like this with.

Cameron: Are you awake?

Sasha: It's 9:00. If I was 70 years old, this might be bedtime.

A smile lifted the corner of his mouth. She'd been businesslike with him this morning, but she didn't seem mad. Maybe they could be just friends, and that was more than he'd had before meeting her.

Cameron: Good. I'm a night owl, so I never know when it's too late to text other people. But I have to show you something.

Sasha: If this is a dick pic...

Cameron: I hope you know me well enough to know I wouldn't do that.

Sasha: Unless I asked you to?

He paused, sucking in a deep breath. She was joking. She probably flirted with guys all the time like this. Time to redirect this conversation back to friend territory. Because that's all they were.

Cameron: Do you want to know what it is or not?

Sasha: You know I'm curious.

Cameron snapped a photo of his spare bedroom, with the comics covering every available surface.

Sasha: Whoa. Your house is messier than I pictured.

Cameron: Normally it's not.

Sasha: I just zoomed in. You're into sci-fi?

Cameron: Yeah. I collect comics. I told you I was a nerd.

Sasha: I don't hold it against you.

The dots of her typing flashed for several moments before the next text appeared.

Sasha: But seriously, that's cool. I've watched some of those TV shows. I'd say invite me over to see your collection, but...

He shook his head. Another cheesy pickup line. She was definitely messing with him now.

Cameron: Anyway. I wanted to thank you.

Sasha: What do you mean?

Cameron: You asked me the other day what things I loved, and I think I'd forgotten about this. Or made myself forget it. But you reminded me it's okay to do things for fun.

A long pause followed his text, and maybe he'd said too much with that statement, which now that he looked at it, sounded kind of like he was referring to their kiss. Which he hadn't been.

Except now he'd thought about it, and it was all he could focus on again. A wave of lust swept through him, picturing her holding her phone, typing her messages to him.

After a minute, she replied.

Sasha: I'm glad you're having fun. Don't forget how again, okay?

It had been fun kissing her. In a terrifying, life-altering way. He'd also had fun chopping onions and rolling knishes and sneaking around in the dark like kids running away from home to a party.

All of it, so much more fun than he'd had in years.

Cameron: I won't forget. Good night.

Sasha: Good night, Mr. Spock.

Chapter 12

On Friday morning, the last day of Cameron's spring break, Sasha punched the bread dough and turned the mass of it over in the oiled steel bowl. After a half-hour rest, it would be ready to roll out for the weekend's orders, which always surpassed the weekdays by a good margin.

The new security camera had been running for forty-eight hours, and there'd been no sign of the vandals. They had a sixth sense, disappearing right when she finally had the means to catch them.

And Cameron would take his camera home with him after today, leaving them back where they'd been before. As soon as he removed the camera, they'd show up again to cause trouble, because that was just how the world worked.

She gave the dough one last punch, slid the plastic wrap over the top, and pushed the bowl away from her across the counter. One more day of having a volunteer helper. Like she'd told Dad from the beginning, the extra pair of hands did help. The dough and filling they'd prepped would last them into next week.

And next week, she and Dad would be back on their own again. She could take care of the work on her own, but it had been nice to have help. From someone who'd said he wanted to be her friend. And then kissed her like they were much more than that.

Maybe it hadn't been the smartest thing, kissing him right after he'd said he wanted to be friends. An unfamiliar tendril of longing had curled through her gut when he'd suggested it, and she hadn't known what to do with that. So she'd gone to her default, the ease of physical communication. But people generally didn't kiss their friends, did they?

He'd surprised her with the intensity of his reaction, too. When she'd pulled him into the storefront, she'd expected a quick kiss, to tease him a little, and then back off. But that wasn't the way it had gone.

Instead, he'd hauled her into him and kissed her so thoroughly, she'd gone hot and liquid, and felt like the top of her head had come off. He'd reacted like he'd never been kissed before, and that was part of the fun, too.

She wouldn't have guessed he had that much fire in him. Or maybe some part of her had known he *did* have it in him and wanted to tease it out.

Whichever it was, it had been electric. Different from any other makeout session. And she'd have been happy to do more, until he'd put a stop to things.

It was the smarter choice, and Cameron struck her as a person who always did the smart thing. Just friends was a good way to go for them. He didn't have time for dating, and she didn't do relationships.

But she also didn't do friendships with men. He'd left her in an unfamiliar space of not knowing where she stood or how to treat him. He wasn't a stranger, and he also wasn't a guy she was planning to hook up with.

So now, he was just…Cameron. The guy she'd gotten to know this last week, and found she could tolerate for long periods of time.

Her mind kept calling forward the feel of his lean, hard body against hers, the sharp smell of his soap in her nose. His hands flexing at her waist. It could be fun to take things further, even if they were only friends with benefits.

He interrupted her train of thought by poking his head in the door. He wore his usual jeans and Henley with the sleeves rolled up, and had his laptop tucked under his arm. The inside of the truck already felt close with the humidity rolling in, but she couldn't picture him switching to something as casual as a T-shirt.

"Hey," he said, giving her a smile that popped his dimple. He'd gotten more attractive somehow in the last week. His face and his eyes had grown on her, and now she couldn't imagine how she'd ever looked at him and only seen a nerdy guy.

"Hey, yourself." She propped a hip on the counter, studying him. "It's your last day."

He cleared his throat, shifting his eyes away from hers. "Yeah. More knishes today?"

She shook her head. "Bialys. We'll roll them out in a half hour."

"Sounds good." He raised the laptop he held. "I brought this. Thought we should check the camera footage today, since it's been a couple days."

"I'm ninety-nine percent certain they haven't been back. But yeah, we should check." She paused, trying to keep her tone neutral as she said the next part. "I guess you'll take the camera back with you today?"

His gaze jerked up. "If you still want it, you can keep using it. I thought... I could come back and check on it in a couple of days?"

"You'd do that? Let us keep it longer?"

"Yeah. I'm breaking a few rules by borrowing it, but I don't think anyone at the lab will miss it in the next few days."

Relief flooded her system. "That would be great. I thought you'd take it away, and then they'd show up right after."

"I wouldn't do that. So, should we go check?"

It wasn't until they were out the door of the truck that she realized he'd said he'd come back again. Ostensibly to check the camera footage. But maybe he wanted to see her again, and that was an excuse. Or maybe she was making things up.

As they walked across the square to Anya's truck, he slanted a glance down at her. "Your dad and Anya seem like they're pretty good friends. Do you think they're romantically involved?"

"What?" She stopped walking and stared up at him. "Of course not."

He shrugged. "Just asking. Your dad's single, right?"

"Yeah, but... No. He's not interested in dating."

But the thought took root as she continued walking. Dad was lonely. He and Anya got along, and she was single, too. Maybe that was part of why Dad had been so insistent on helping defend her truck. He'd always been community-minded, but he'd put his own safety on the line for Anya.

She knocked on Anya's door, and the older woman opened

it. She wore a dark orange tunic over black pants today, her hair piled on top of her head in a messy bun.

"Good morning. You brought your friend."

"Nice to see you again," Cameron told her.

"We were hoping we could check the camera footage," Sasha explained.

"Of course. Come on in."

She and Cameron climbed the steps into the truck, and Cameron busied himself removing the memory card from the camera and inserting it into his laptop. As he uploaded the footage to his hard drive, Sasha turned to Anya, unable to hide her curiosity.

"Are you and Dad dating?" she blurted. She'd never been good at subtlety.

"Ha!" A laugh burst out of the older woman, her wide smile showing all her teeth, including a couple of gold ones in the back. "Where did you get that idea?"

Sasha shot Cameron a look, and he ducked his head, looking extra busy with his laptop.

"It just occurred to me. I mean, you guys *have* spent a lot of time together recently, and I wouldn't be surprised if—"

"Sasha." Anya laid a hand on her arm. "Your dad and I aren't dating. Neither one of us wants that."

"You don't?"

"Come sit for a minute." Anya gestured for her to go out the front door, and they sat on the steps side by side.

Now that she'd asked her rash question, she wanted to take it back. But a small part of her wanted it to be true. For Dad to have someone to care about besides her.

"I'm sorry if that was too nosy," she said.

The older woman shook her head. "Not at all. I thought

122

you might be more comfortable talking out here, where your friend can't listen in."

Anya tilted her head to one side, then the other, a unique gesture she did when she was thinking hard about something.

"Sasha. Your dad… He's a wonderful friend to me. But he's never stopped loving your mother. Not for one day."

Unexpected tears burned her eyes. "I know that."

She'd always known it, but hearing the other woman say it made it that much more obvious.

"I don't think he'll ever love someone again in that way. And that's okay. There's all this pressure when you get divorced or widowed to find the next person. But that's not how hearts work."

"I know that, too." A lifetime of watching Dad remember Mom as if she was still there had taught her as much.

"And as for me," Anya continued, "I never wanted to marry in the first place. There were…family pressures on me to do it, and so I did. And of course, I've never regretted having Kiran. He's the light of my life. But getting divorced was the best thing that ever happened to me. I'm not interested in romantic relationships. At all."

"I get that."

Anya's large brown eyes glowed with warmth. "Your dad is a good man. We enjoy each other's company, and for that, I'm grateful. I hope that's okay with you?"

"Of course it's okay. I'm glad he has a friend."

"I'm glad, too."

Cameron poked his head out the door, looking uncomfortable.

"I got all the footage uploaded. I can wait in here, if you want to keep talking?"

123

"No, it's okay." Sasha swiped at her eyes with the back of her hand and stood. "We have to get back to the dough."

"Come back anytime," Anya told them.

"It's okay if leave the camera here for another few days?" she asked.

"However long you need. I'm glad we have a chance to catch them on film."

Anya waved them off, and they headed back across the square.

"I'm sorry," Cameron said when they were out of earshot. "I didn't mean to start anything."

"No, it's okay. I'm glad I asked. I know Dad's been lonely, and it makes me feel better to know he has a friend."

"Friends are good." Cameron shot an unreadable look at her. "When we get back to the truck, I'll go through the footage more carefully, but a quick scan didn't show anything."

"Yeah. I figured. Thanks again for letting us borrow it." At the truck door, she paused with her hand on the knob. "You've done a lot more to help me out than I have you at this point."

"That's not true." His eyes scanned her face. "You helped me remember what fun is."

Her heart accelerated, remembering the other night. "I guess your life was pretty boring before."

"It was." He nodded. "Sasha… If the camera does ever get footage, do you know who you'll take it to? Do you have a way to report it?"

"Yeah. I mentioned to Matt that we got a new camera at my last session. I didn't tell him you've been helping me out," she added quickly, at the look of alarm on his face. "Don't worry, I won't tell your coworkers you're here, or why. I remember the deal."

He shook his head, looking rueful. "I'm not sure the deal matters anymore."

"Well, I promised I wouldn't tell anyone about your…"

"Terrible job performance?" he supplied.

"Yeah, about that. But it wasn't your fault. You were tired."

"I was worse than tired. I believe 'burnout' is the correct term. But what did Matt tell you to do?"

"He gave me a contact at the police department. He said to take any evidence to them, and it might even help clear my record of charges, if I had proof of ongoing vandalism."

"That would be amazing."

"I'm not even letting myself hope for that right now. All I want is for them to leave Dad and Anya alone."

"We'll get the footage." He sounded more confident than she felt. "Then you'll take down the bad guys with…the power of knowledge." He waggled his eyebrows dramatically.

"Cameron. That is the most ridiculous thing I've ever heard."

He folded his arms across his chest, pulling the laptop to him with a knowing smile. "Just wait. You'll see what the right information can do."

"All right. And until then, you're about to see the power of twenty pounds of bread dough."

They were both laughing as they climbed the RV steps and dove into rolling out the bialys, placing a scoop of onion and poppyseed filling into the center of each roll. They laughed more when Cameron set a roll down too hard into a pile of flour, exploding a white cloud of powder onto his face.

Having a friend was a very nice thing. But now their time together was almost over. She'd see him maybe one more time next week, when he came to check the camera. Maybe she'd catch a glimpse of him at The Well Space, if he still worked late nights.

It didn't feel like enough. And maybe he felt the same way, because he took longer than usual doing the dishes, stretching out the task of drying and putting away the sheet pans until much later than normal.

When he had nothing left to do, he gathered his laptop and went to the door, hesitating there. What did she do now? Shake his hand?

"Thank you for your help—"

"I had a good time—"

They both spoke at the same time, then broke off into awkward silence.

Cameron cleared his throat. "Thanks for letting me help out this week. It was a much better spring break than I could have dreamed up on my own."

"I'm working the night shift tomorrow," she said, before she could think better of it. "If you wanted to come back."

"I could do that," he said quickly.

Her eyes flew up to meet his. This was not him doing her a favor or part of their deal. This was him coming back because he wanted to.

"Thanks. Saturday nights are the busiest. So that would be really helpful."

She kept her tone casual, as if he was any other volunteer coming by to help out. But her heart rate had picked up. She was never nervous around men. Not even burly, two-hundred-pound men who wanted to do her bodily harm. She rubbed her damp palms on her jeans.

"What time should I come by?" he asked.

"5:00. Before the evening rush."

"I'll be here." He hesitated for a moment, as if he was about to say something else, then shook his head and ducked out the door.

Maybe he just wanted to be friends. But he hadn't wanted to say goodbye, either. They'd have more time together.

She hummed as she put the first trays of rolls into the convection oven.

Dad kicked open the door with a foot a moment later, lugging a forty-pound bag of flour in his arms.

"You're in a good mood today," he greeted her. "Why are you singing?"

"It's nice weather today. Spring is here, and we're about to catch some criminals."

"Humph." He dropped the flour on the counter beside her. "These look uneven," he added, inspecting the trays of bialys.

"Yeah, it was only Cameron's second time on those."

Dad raised a brow at her. "How long is he helping out, anyway?"

"One more day. Actually, I was thinking you could take tomorrow night off, since he's coming to help out."

Dad's brows went down. "I don't need a night off."

"We could argue about this for the next hour. Or, you could take the time to do something fun. See a movie. Hang out with a friend."

Dad opened his mouth to interrupt, but she plowed on.

"Speaking of friends, Anya was telling me this morning how you guys have been hanging out more often. She's really glad to have you around."

Dad's expression softened. "She is good company. Always brings me lunch after you leave."

"So maybe sometime you'll hang out together outside of work. As friends. I know you don't want anything more than that, but friends are good to have."

Dad narrowed his eyes at her, considering. "I'll think about it. But I don't want to leave you alone here at night, not with the possibility of—"

"I won't be alone, I told you. Cameron will be helping out. Hey." She put a hand on his arm, inspiration striking. "What if you helped at Anya's on Saturday? You'd be nearby in case I needed you, but you'd get away from the truck for a night. And you'd get to hang out with a friend. Plus, you could keep an eye on the security camera."

"Maybe," he deflected. "I don't suppose we got anything yet."

"No, we didn't. But Cameron's lending it to us for another week."

Dad's eyebrow went up. "That's a nice offer. And you want to be alone with him on Saturday. Interesting."

"Dad, stop."

He gave a long-suffering sigh. "Fine. I will help Anya on Saturday night. And you can be alone here with your *friend*." He put special emphasis on the last word.

She grabbed her bag and ducked out the door to go to work. It had been a long time since she'd been embarrassed in front of Dad. And she'd never been good at hiding her feelings the way some people were.

Dad had seen through her, and Cameron probably could, too. Just friends, she told herself in the car, and turned up the volume on her music.

Chapter 13

C ameron inhaled the warm, lilac-scented breeze as he made his way across the square. The area was busy on a Saturday night, a lot busier than it had been all week. The first shades of twilight darkened the sky in the early spring evening.

A good night to go out, after the record snowstorms they'd had in February this year, and everyone else in town seemed to agree, because the place was packed. Couples and families with children roamed the renovated downtown area, stopping to browse at storefronts which stayed open later on weekend evenings. The movie theater around the block had a line out the door, and the ice cream parlor looked full through the glass windows.

The food trucks lining the block were doing a brisk business, some with lines four or five people deep. Cameron hurried over to the knish truck. The side window was open, and as he approached, Sasha was handing a paper bag of knishes to a customer.

"Hey. You made it," she called down to him.

"You should have told me to come earlier." He jogged up the steps and joined her inside. When she turned to face him, flashing him a smile, his heart flip-flopped inside his chest.

She wore a black tank top tonight, and her usual white apron tied at her waist over black ripped jeans. In the waning light, her silver piercings winked, and the happiness in her expression stopped him in his tracks.

She was happy to see him. Most people were not happy at the sight of him, and he was never the life of the party.

Sasha's smile drew him like moths to the fairy lights strung around the outside of the truck, and he approached her, an answering smile taking over his face.

"No need for you to get here any earlier," she said. "It's slow right now."

"This is slow?"

"Oh, yeah. But it's about to pick up. I forgot you've never been here when we're open. Slow would be a Tuesday morning at 11:00. Right now, the party's about to start."

"Show me what to do, then."

After he washed his hands and put on an apron, she walked him through the process of bagging the knishes for customers, adding silverware and condiments, and transferring batches of the pastries in and out of the oven.

"I'll set the oven timers and run the register up front," she told him. "You can bag the product and bake."

"Fine with me."

"And let me know if you can't keep up. Dad's helping Anya tonight, but I'm sure he'd come back if we needed him. I promised him we wouldn't, though."

She averted her gaze from his, looking almost shy for a

minute.

"I can keep up," he told her.

He could keep up with any amount of work. On Monday, his spring break would be over, and it would be time to go back to his real life, his real work. In the past, he would have looked forward to getting back.

In the past, he never would have stopped working during spring break at all. He would have carried on with the outrageous hours and been grateful for a return to the normal routine when break was over.

Forty-eight hours from now, he'd slide back into his habits of working late, punishing his body and mind with long hours, and for what? School had felt pointless for weeks now. A joyless, colorless pursuit.

This week hadn't been colorless, though. He didn't want it to be over. He'd jumped at the chance, any chance, to come back here again. The camera was another excuse he'd use to come back in a few days.

As for tonight, he had no excuse. Other than wanting to see Sasha again.

He stood by her side, listening to her take the next few orders, a sense of lightness buzzing under his skin. He bagged hot pastries, folded the paper bags over, and sealed them with a sticker before handing them down to the customers. He brushed against Sasha's arm as she tapped the screen of the register, and she gave him another warm look.

Her glossy, dark hair swung around her chin as she turned between the countertop and the register, her hands moving in a practiced series of actions. She was sweating lightly in the warm evening, with the ovens blazing inside the truck. The smell of caramelized onions filled the small space, and underneath it, the smell of her shampoo was floral and sweet.

A bubble of feeling expanded in his chest, the result of too much good sensory input. Her hip bumping his as they worked side by side. The flash of her nose ring in the deepening dusk.

At one point, they had a line of ten people waiting, and she laughed as she watched him open a paper bag in each hand, loading up customer orders two at a time.

"You're a machine," she said.

"I'm a hard worker."

But that wasn't all he was, anymore. He *was* a hard worker, but he could feel joy and do work at the same time.

A few minutes after 8:00, Kiran came jogging over from the momo truck across the square. The gangly teenager had long limbs and deep brown skin, and he gave Sasha a crooked smile as he approached.

"Mom says I should come check on you. And also tell you Alexei is going crazy, seeing all the customers waiting over here. She said you should tell me something reassuring, like everything is fine, or he will come over here and make a nuisance of himself."

"Tell him everything is fine, because it is," Sasha replied. "Tell him I said to go see a movie."

Kiran's grin widened. "I don't think he'll do that. Also, Mom said to tell you someone saw the vandals earlier this afternoon. They drove by on Second Street, then sped away. No one's seen them again tonight, though."

Cameron's gut twisted. In his enjoyment of the evening, he'd almost forgotten about the camera and the danger Sasha's neighborhood faced.

Next to him, Sasha's spine straightened. "They could come back later."

Kiran cocked his head to the side. "I know. That's one more reason Alexei is making a pain of himself right now. He's worried about you."

"Tell him not to worry," Cameron told the younger man. "She's not alone, and I won't leave her alone after we close."

Sasha tossed six knishes into a bag and handed them to Kiran through the window.

"These are for you and your mom. Payment for putting up with a grumpy old man."

"I'm starting to suspect he does it for show," Kiran said.

"Now you're getting it." She gave Kiran a bright smile, but after the boy loped away, Sasha turned to him, her expression sobering.

"Maybe it'll be tonight."

There was no need for her to explain what she meant. Another sliver of unease went through him.

"Maybe so. But if it's tonight, we'll get footage. No one has to do anything but wait for them to incriminate themselves and leave."

She drew in a deep inhale. "Right now, I'm trying to remember all the anger management techniques Matt has taught me so far."

"Are they working?"

Her expression turned thoughtful. "I don't know yet. To be honest, I wasn't sure I was going to try that hard in therapy. Or at all. But he's been having me try simple things first. Like taking deep breaths before I take action. Naming my emotions. Real sophisticated stuff."

"Hey, the simple things work best sometimes."

She frowned. "I'm starting to wonder if I should take therapy more seriously. I get angry, and I need to own that. I'm an angry person, Cameron."

"No," he said, his tone firm. "You're a happy person. A person who's had shitty things happen to them, things that would make anyone feel angry. But that's not who you are."

"You think so?" Her eyes sparkled up at him, and his hands itched to reach for her. But they were interrupted by another wave of customers and turned back to their assigned jobs.

Which was a good thing. If customers hadn't appeared, he might have reached for her and pulled her into his arms, which had proved dangerous last time.

Just friends—that was all they were. Friends who might be somewhat attracted to one another, but who could support each other all the same. He was a friend who remembered what her hair smelled like. The taste of her breath haunted him at night when he couldn't sleep.

The best and smartest thing for them, as friends, was to respect their mutual boundaries. But sometimes, he wished he didn't care so much about rules.

By 10:00, customer traffic had slowed, and they took a break, sitting on the steps to breathe in the cool night air, eating bialys and drinking full-sugar orange soda. The syrupy sweetness chased the burn down his throat.

"Almost done," she told him. "We close at 11:00, but it'll be getting quieter now."

"I see that."

Already, foot traffic had lessened. Streetlights lit the bright square, but as he scanned the space, he saw all the dark corners and hidden alcoves where someone with bad intentions might hide.

The night was quiet so far, matching the peace in his brain. His brain was never quiet, except around her.

Kiran jogged over to tell them Alexei was driving Anya home in an hour, and Sasha promised to lock up the truck. She reassured the boy three times that she wouldn't be alone all evening.

After Kiran left again, Sasha leaned back with her hands on the steps behind her, studying the night sky.

"You can't see the stars very well with the street lights. But Sagittarius is over there." She pointed at a spot in the sky to the left of them.

"I forgot you're into astrology."

"I have a tattoo of Aries on my hip. Maybe you'll see it sometime," she added, bumping him with her shoulder.

He swallowed, heat lighting up his veins. "That sounds like a pickup line."

She turned to face him, eyes shining in the darkness. "Would it work, if it was?"

"Uh. It might."

Words swirled out of his brain, water down a drain. Along with all the reasons why this would be a bad idea. He couldn't seem to catch hold of the threads of why they shouldn't.

He'd told himself friends was the smart option. But he wasn't feeling very smart right now.

"You know, you've never told me your birthday," she said. "I have to know your sign, too. To know if being friends with you is a bad idea."

It took him a minute to come up with the date.

"February 17th."

"Hmm. Aquarius. That tracks. Wait a minute." She straightened, pulled her phone out of her pocket, and opened her calendar app. "Wait a minute. The night we met was February 17th."

"It was?"

His innocent tone didn't fool her, though.

"Are you telling me you were working late, and fell asleep exhausted on someone else's desk, and it was also your *birthday*?"

Her tone rose in outrage on the last word, and he had no good reply.

"I…didn't really think much about it?"

"So you turned what, twenty-eight—"

"Twenty-nine."

"You turned twenty-nine asleep at a desk. At work."

"I mean, technically, I was home before midnight. So I spent part of my birthday at home."

"Cameron. I say this with all due respect. But what the fuck."

A laugh burst out of him, taking him over from the inside. More of that light feeling filled his head, expanding into his chest.

"You have an elegant way of putting things," he told her when he'd stopped laughing.

"And you have a problem with overworking yourself," she grumbled.

"I do." He sobered and met her gaze. "But at least I can admit it now. I had fun this week, not working with you."

"So all this is not working?" She gestured to the food truck behind them.

"It's work, but it's fun. Maybe because of the company."

Her expression warmed. "Yeah. Company is good. Nicer than I'd have thought."

Their eyes held a beat too long, and for a half second, he thought she'd kiss him again, but then two women wandered over to order food, breaking the spell.

136

"I can help you out," Sasha told them, jumping to her feet and hurrying back inside.

Cameron rose slowly, brushing off his jeans. Just because it seemed like they were about to kiss, didn't mean they would have. She'd been flirting with him, but that didn't mean anything.

He was overthinking things, as usual. When he joined her behind the counter, she was all business, handing the customers their food and sending them off with a wave.

They had less than an hour until close, and after that, their time together was over. Unless something happened to change that.

After the customers wandered off, he cleared his throat. "I'll get started on the dishes."

"There aren't too many. Mostly the baking sheets. I'll help you in a few, after I close the register."

She busied herself with the tasks of closing, and he filled the dish sink, and wondered how he was ever going to walk away after tonight.

Chapter 14

Cameron had been quiet for the last half hour, ever since he'd retreated to the dish sink. When he got quiet like that, he was thinking about something. Out on the steps, they'd seemed close to kissing. But Cameron liked to overthink, and maybe he was talking himself out of it. A sliver of disappointment went through her at the thought.

Why she was disappointed, she wouldn't examine too closely. They'd had a fun week. They'd shared an explosive kiss. And then they'd decided to be friends.

Still, his expression had been warm and open, out there on the steps. His eyes had locked onto hers and held, inviting her to push the envelope, to see what would happen. He could be fun to push.

He needed more fun in his life, and she could give that to him. It didn't have to be more complicated than friends with benefits.

She rolled the metal covering down over the service window at 11:00 sharp—official closing time. She started the register's shutdown sequence and pulled out the change drawer to count the cash.

In her peripheral vision, she watched Cameron work, sleeves rolled up and hands deep in the soapy water. He was too serious. But he also had a sense of humor. He got her jokes, which were too abrasive for some people. He got her, period.

She wanted him more than she'd wanted other guys, maybe because of the false sense of closeness they'd developed over the last week. He'd met her family, spent time at her workplace. She'd let him in closer than arm's length, which was more than she'd allowed other guys. For the first time, she was attracted to more than a man's body.

He also smelled nice and kissed really filthy, and maybe it was true what people said, that the quiet ones had a lot more going on under the surface.

After she'd finished balancing the register, she slid the curtain aside and glanced around the square. The space was dark and getting quieter, the last few vendors taking out the trash and closing down for the night. The sound of an outdoor concert drifted over from a few blocks away, along with the scent of smoke from a nearby restaurant's outdoor fire pit.

A few people still wandered the neighborhood, enjoying the warm evening. Anyone thinking about making trouble would surely avoid the neighborhood on such a busy night.

She took out the garbage, swept the steps, and locked the door behind her as she came back inside. Cameron was unloading the last of the trays from the rinse sink, a sheen of sweat on his forehead from the hot water and the humid air. He was focused on the task, a small frown of concentration on his forehead.

She grabbed a dish towel and went to stand by him, moving

into his space like she'd done a couple of times earlier this evening.

When you wanted to feel out an opponent, the smartest thing to do was gauge their reaction, using your powers of observation about their body language. As her hip bumped against his, Cameron didn't move away. He let her make contact.

She reached across him for a baking sheet, brushing her torso against his arm. His sharp indrawn breath told her everything he wasn't saying. Her pulse throbbed, because this was the fun part, the part where she could tease, see how far she could push him before something happened.

Maybe that something was him telling her he didn't want this. But maybe that something would be a lot more fun. Blood rushed in her ears, part adrenaline and part excitement. The vibe he was giving off didn't say "friends."

She reached across him again to place her baking sheet on the rack above his head, letting her body make contact with his again, lingering a moment longer than last time. His hand froze on the pan he'd been drying.

"What are you doing?" He shook his head. "Don't answer that. I think I already know."

Slowly, she lowered from her tiptoes back to the floor. "I think I'm moving into your personal space. Want me to stop?"

He set down his dish towel on the counter, his chest rising and falling. He shut his eyes for a moment, and maybe she'd pushed him too far. Maybe this was too much for her controlled, reserved guy.

She took a step back, giving him room to decide. "Hey, it's okay if you don't want to—"

"No." His hand snagged the side of her tank top and pulled

her closer, knocking her off balance enough that her torso crashed into his, and she was never caught off guard by an opponent, but he shocked the hell out of her when his mouth came down on hers.

With a helpless, rough sound, his mouth moved on hers urgently, while his palms slid up her back, over her exposed shoulder blades. His hands were hot, and she shivered, threading her arms around his neck. He tasted like the orange soda he'd drunk, and against her chest, his heart beat hard enough to feel through two layers of fabric.

This was as good as she'd remembered. In the last few days, she'd questioned whether their first kiss had really been that hot, and now she had the answer. It was better, because he tasted and felt real and solid, like something she could depend on, for the first time in ever.

She pushed him back against the counter and took more. Her hands went under his shirt, feeling the hard muscles of his abdomen twitch under her fingers. He wore a T-shirt under the Henley, which was probably why his skin felt so deliciously hot under her fingertips. A light dusting of hair covered his taut abdomen, forming a trail leading into the waistband of his jeans.

She flicked open the button and palmed the front of his fly, and it really was true the quiet ones had a lot going on under the surface, because Cameron was packing a lot below the belt. A ripple of anticipation went through her as she traced the shape.

He ripped his mouth away from hers on a gasp.

"Too much?" she asked, tipping her face up to his.

In the trailer's dim light, she could make out the flush high on his cheekbones, his mouth wet from kisses and his eyes unfocused. He looked delicious, and more than a little confused.

"It's not too much." He sucked in another breath. "It's just…" He shook his head.

"What?"

"Would you believe me if I said it's never been like this for me before?" His mouth twisted up in a rueful half smile. "It sounds like a line, but it's true."

She leaned into him, bringing their mouths within kissing distance again. "It's never been like what?"

He shoved a hand through his curls. "I feel like I'm going crazy. Like if I don't do this, I'll go crazy. This isn't how I am."

Satisfaction rushed through her. "But you like it?"

"Yeah. I like it." His pupils darkened as he gazed down at her.

"Then why's it so crazy? It's just having fun together."

His brows went down, and she could almost see his brain struggling to kick in.

"You know the reasons why. We agreed on being friends. Because…" He trailed off, looking lost.

"Because I don't do relationships. And you don't have time for one. I remember." She leaned closer. "Haven't you ever heard of friends with benefits?"

"I don't…" He drew in a breath. "That's not something I've ever done."

"You're a relationship kind of guy."

"I guess, if you'd asked me a week ago, I'd have said yes. But like I said, I'm not acting like I normally do right now. I must be out of my mind."

"Stop thinking about what happens after. Think about now. What do you want right now?"

His eyes darkened further. "I want you. I don't have to tell you that."

She ran her fingers down his front, delighting in the shiver he couldn't hide.

"So what would happen if you let yourself have what you want? Let us both have what we want?" she asked softly, uncertain what his answer would be.

He took in a shuddering inhale. "I think... I think that would be acceptable."

"Acceptable." She flattened her palm against his abdomen and slid it up under the hem of his shirt.

He cleared his throat. "More than acceptable. Good. A great idea."

She grinned up at him, and his answering smile lit her up inside.

"Good. Come on, then."

"Where are we going?"

"To bed. It's up front, above the driver's seat." She grabbed his hand and shot him another smile over her shoulder as she pulled them forward.

"Oh, God."

"What?"

"I kept trying not to look up there, the whole time we've been working here together."

"Why not?"

He almost tripped over his shoes as they crossed the small space. "Because I wanted you, and I couldn't let myself think about the fact that there was a bed six feet away from us."

"Sometimes it's good to think about things." She stopped at the base of the short ladder leading up to the bunk, snagged the front of his shirt, and pulled him down into another kiss.

The moan that came out of him didn't sound like any sound she'd heard come out of his mouth. It was desperate, wild.

She threaded her hands into his hair, pulled him closer, and kissed him until they were both out of breath. She ripped her mouth from his.

"Up," she told him. "You won't be able to stand up there, so you might as well lie down."

"Oh, God." But he did what she told him to do, and scaled the ladder, and she followed him up.

"You keep saying that, and I'll get a big head."

He shifted his weight to the far side of the bunk, leaning his back against the wall, legs extended in front of him. The narrow space held a full-size mattress with blankets, barely enough room for both of them.

"Take your shirt off," she ordered. "But leave the glasses on." It was hot in the small space, and besides, she'd been dying to see him.

He complied, his eyes meeting hers before and after the shirt slid over his head. He was silent, his eyes glittering in the dim light of the street lamp that shone through the rectangular window.

He looked debauched, all smooth skin and wild hair, the bulge in the front of his jeans all for her. He was hers for now, for tonight, and that was enough.

She crawled over to him and straddled his lap. At the contact, he hissed in a breath through his teeth. She stripped her tank top and bra over her head with brisk efficiency and kissed him again, slow and thorough. His hands hovered at her waist, as if waiting for permission to do more. She grabbed them, putting one hand on her breast and the other on her ass.

He groaned, his head dropping forward into her neck like

a puppet with the strings cut. His kisses took on urgency as his mouth roamed her neck, and down her torso. She moved over him, feeling the fire ignite in her blood. His hands had lost their sense of propriety now, palming her hips, stroking up her back. When his mouth closed over her breast, she let her head fall back at the bolt of heat that shot through her.

This was the part of sex she loved the most, the part where the world fell away, and there was only a firestorm of heat and feeling and movement. And this time it was more, better somehow, because he needed this, and he'd let her give it to him. Because he hadn't felt this way with anyone else, but he'd let himself go with her. And she'd trusted him to get close.

She pushed the length of her body against him, and he strained up into her. Abruptly, the kissing wasn't enough. Both of them needed more. She put a palm on his chest, pushing him away, and he stared up at her.

"Why is it like this with you?" He looked confused, out of breath.

"It's good?"

"So good. But you have to show me what you want. It's been a while for me, and I don't want to mess this up for you."

"What I want…" She slid off his lap, considering her options, thinking of what would drive him the most insane, and take her along for the ride. Carefully, she lowered his zipper, reveling in the way his chest pumped up and down as if he'd been running.

"I think I want to suck you…"

"Oh, God."

"…And then I want you inside me. Okay?"

He nodded vigorously, seeming incapable of speech as she slid down his body. The groan he let out as her mouth closed around him was incautiously loud. She raised her head.

"There are still people outside. Might want to be quieter."

Then she went back to the task of making him lose his mind. He couldn't stop his hips pitching off the mattress, though he seemed to be trying, his back arching as she used all her favorite tricks on him. This was the most fun she'd had in forever, his unguarded reactions stoking the fever building inside her until she slid her hand under her waistband, rubbing herself through her underwear as she sucked him.

She could come like this, and so could he, if the continuous stream of moans coming from him was any indicator. But she wasn't done having fun with him yet.

She rolled off of him, slid out of her jeans and underwear, and reached for her wallet. She looked up to find him watching her with hot eyes. He looked predatory, like he might jump on her, an expression she'd never expected to see on his thoughtful face. Some other time, maybe they could explore that impulse. But for now…

"You keep condoms in your wallet," he said.

"Of course." She slid one out, ripped it open, and straddled his legs. "Aren't you glad I do?"

"I am. Sasha, I am…not going to last very long."

"It's okay. I'm not going to, either."

"I didn't get to touch you as much as I wanted. I want to do that to you. What you did to me."

"Maybe some other time. For now—"

He hissed in a breath as she rolled the condom on and positioned the head of his erection at her entrance.

"For now, this is what I want." She sank down, her eyes falling shut as the hot substance of his erection filled her. When he was fully inside, she moved slowly, making slight adjustments to find the perfect angle.

Cameron's mouth had fallen open, and she kissed him. His returning kiss was messy, verging on desperate. She wanted him so far past desperate he wouldn't remember his own name. She was on her way there herself.

He felt good inside her, hot and full and perfect. But also strangely right, and familiar, even though they'd never done this before. Like he was meant to be there. His hands were back on her hips, unconsciously trying to speed her motions, but she didn't, not yet. Both of them could wait a little longer. The buildup was half the fun.

Her thighs flexed around him, feeling all the best parts of them press together. He was a good partner, responsive to her movements, matching her and driving her higher. He let her have control, but he was there with her at every step, pushing her arousal to a breaking point. She should've known he'd be unselfish in bed, helping her find her release.

The storm brewing inside her thrashed, waiting to be let loose, demanding more, and now. She held onto his shoulders and let herself go, rising and falling over him in the fast, urgent rhythm her body demanded. The tension inside her was close to the breaking point, roaring with heat.

Cameron went rigid beneath her, his head going back against the wall, mouth open. His breath caught in his throat, but no sound came out of him. Beneath her, his body racked with the first wave of his release, and it was enough to pitch her over the edge.

Hot waves of satisfaction rolled through her, amplified by the fact that Cameron appeared to be still coming. For what felt like an endless minute, his body twitched underneath her with aftershocks before falling still. His eyes were shut, his chest pumping up and down.

She fell against his torso, which was hot and sheened with sweat, catching her breath. That had been better than any sex she'd had in a long time. Maybe ever. She wouldn't mind a repeat, even though she didn't do repeats with the same guy.

It should worry her that she could see herself wanting more of this, wanting more with him. She'd need to be careful and not sleep with him too many times in a row, or she might start to get attached, or think this meant something it didn't.

Things like supportive, long-term relationships didn't happen for her, much as they seemed to work out for other people.

She lifted her head and looked down at him. He still hadn't opened his eyes, but his breathing had slowed. He looked relaxed, and also fucked out, and a sliver of pride went through her as she admired her handiwork.

"Cameron."

"Unh."

"Are you okay?"

"Uh-huh."

A smile she couldn't stop spread across her face. "Do you remember your own name?"

"Very funny. It's George, by the way." He patted her hip, then let his hand fall to the blankets.

"Are you falling asleep?"

"No," he said, but his body had gone even more relaxed and boneless beneath hers. She climbed off him, disposed of the condom, and flicked the blanket up over his body. She slid in next to him, tucking her head under his shoulder and slinging an arm across his waist.

She didn't usually sleep with men after sex, either. But she could make an exception, just this once, for an hour or two.

Cameron was already out cold, his breath even in sleep. The

148

soft rise and fall of his chest lulled her under, too, along with the unfamiliar feeling that somehow, this was right where she was supposed to be.

Chapter 15

Cameron woke to movement on the mattress and opened his eyes to see Sasha pulling her shirt on. He sat up in a rush, but his muscles felt loose and uncoordinated, his eyes heavy.

"I fell asleep," he said.

She tossed a smile over her shoulder. "Yep. We only slept about an hour, though. It's quarter to 1:00."

"I'm sorry."

"Don't be. It was fun. We should do it again sometime."

Her tone was light and easy, almost cheerful. Something was off with her, though. It reminded him of their first kiss, how quickly she'd retreated when he'd said they were better off as friends.

They should do it again sometime. As if 'it' was a game of chess, and not the hottest sex of his life. For a minute, toward the end, he'd been sure he would pass out from pleasure. Surely, his consciousness couldn't sustain that much dopamine.

But maybe she did this all the time, the casual sex thing.

Maybe it hadn't been anything unusual for her. The thought sent a chill through his gut, and he sat up.

"Do it again sometime," he repeated. He shook his head, trying to bring his fuzzy brain back online. He patted the mattress until he located his boxer briefs and jeans, and pulled them on.

"Yeah. I thought it was fun. Don't you want to?" She turned halfway on the mattress, watching as he did up his fly. She sounded too damn casual for the way he was feeling, which was like someone had ripped a hole in his chest and flooded him with messy, uncertain feelings.

"It's not that I don't want to. Sasha. That was…"

"It was pretty good, right?" The corner of her mouth kicked up.

"It was better than good. You have to know that already." He fought the urge to reach for her hand, because she might not want that. She had her clothes back on, and she looked ready to climb down the ladder in a moment. She'd drive off, and this whole evening would be a memory for her. Another of her casual flings.

"Then what's the problem? We both had fun. We can keep having fun if you want to. And if you don't, that's okay, too." She lifted her shoulder in a shrug.

He frowned, his brain furiously trying to catch up. "Earlier, you said this was friends with benefits. Is that what you want?"

She gave a quick nod before her gaze slid away from his, but not before he saw something there. A flash of nerves. It was possible she felt a small portion of what he was feeling right now, and she was covering it up with an attempt to act casual. The question was, could he match that, pretend to feel casual when his insides were a confusing riot?

151

"I mean, usually I like to keep things no-strings with guys," she added. "I just thought… If you wanted to see each other again, we could. But we don't have to."

So she'd never been in a serious relationship, and maybe still wasn't looking for one. He had school and work hanging over his head, and keeping things casual made the most sense for him, too.

But he wasn't feeling casual and friendly. He gave in to the urge to reach for her, placing a hand on her shoulder, feeling the smooth skin over her colorful ink. He hadn't gotten to touch and explore her enough. It had been over too quickly. She was so bright and hot, he'd burst into flames at her nearness. And he wanted to do it again.

"I do want to see you again." His voice came out rough, and he cleared his throat. "But I have to be honest with you. I can try no-strings, but it's not really… I'm not sure I'm built that way. It might not work for me."

She held his gaze, her eyes solemn and deep.

"Haven't you ever wanted to try for more with a guy?" he asked.

"No. I haven't." She shook her head, but again, her expression shifted. For a second, she looked sad, and he'd bet anything she had thought about it. Thought about it, but never let herself try.

"Okay." He sucked in a deep breath. "Then we'll do casual. I'd rather see you than not see you."

"Me too." Her voice sounded softer than usual, almost shy, which wasn't like her at all.

"I'll text you, then."

"All right." She swung a leg over the edge of the loft and climbed down the ladder. He walked her to her car, and she

152

gave him a brief hug goodbye, which somehow touched a nerve in the center of his chest.

He drove home and fell into bed, where his brain replayed the evening over and over. He'd been helpless, pulled under the tide of feeling like a surfer in a monster wave.

It made no sense, because he wasn't like that with emotions, but it had happened. And if it happened once, it could happen with her again. He wasn't going to be able to keep it casual around her, like they were just acquaintances who fucked. She'd blown his mind and then walked away into the night, as if it was nothing.

He was in way over his head with this. She was dangerous to his good sense, to everything he should be focusing on right now. But he couldn't stop it, either. She wanted to see him again, and he'd been unable to say no. And that in itself was scary.

She'd owned him tonight, plain and simple. He fell asleep with her scent still in his nose and one hand over his heart.

* * *

Monday mornings at The Well Space were always busy, and the Monday after spring break was no exception. Cameron booted up his laptop, where no doubt several hundred emails awaited him. He hadn't checked the scheduling software, either, something he normally did on a Sunday night before work.

He'd been preoccupied yesterday. Unable to focus. Twenty-four hours was too soon for casual friends to call or text, so instead, he'd paced his apartment, gone through more of his comic collection, and in general, not gotten anything done. He'd pay for it today.

He also hadn't looked at his schoolwork. Not once all weekend. Every time he'd looked at his laptop, the thread of tension pulled tighter in his stomach. It had been easier to enjoy mornings with Sasha, his bizarre new habit of taking an afternoon nap, and then spend the evenings sorting through comics.

He had a list of new issues he wanted to add to his growing collection, and a new cataloging system was shaping up in his mind. Whenever he got the courage to boot up his computer.

Which was now. He winced at the total number of unread emails in his inbox and flipped open the scheduling software. Ben had no appointment first thing this morning, so maybe he'd come in an hour late, something he'd been doing since he'd gotten married, and in the process, discovered how to relax. Maybe Cameron should ask him for lessons.

As if he'd been summoned, Ben appeared at the top of the stairs at the third-floor landing, dressed in his usual three-piece suit and tie. His formality intimidated a lot of people, but he'd been dealing with a lot of his own demons in the last year.

Before he'd been hired at The Well Space, Cameron had idolized Ben and the clinic. Ben's books and the clinic's unique setup made it his number one choice of place to work. When an admin assistant job had opened up, he'd jumped at it as a way to get his foot in the door.

Now he knew his boss was only human, which made him more relatable and, impossibly, made Cameron respect the man more. If he didn't get the job here after graduation, there was no plan B.

"You're back from break," Ben greeted him, picking up the stack of mail on Cameron's desk. "How was your week?"

Crazy. I volunteered in a food truck and developed a massive crush on the woman who works there. Who also happens to be a client at the clinic.

"It was good," he said. "Good to get away for a while, spend some time at home."

Ben raised a brow. "You didn't travel?"

"No, I stayed in town. Worked on some projects."

"Let me guess. For school."

"Actually, no." He averted his eyes from his boss's sharp gaze. "I haven't been on top of my schoolwork lately."

"That's not like you." Ben paused, seeming to consider his words. "Can we chat in my office? I have something I've been meaning to ask you about."

"Of course." Cameron's stomach dropped because being asked into Ben's office was not a great sign. He wasn't a harsh boss, but he got right to the point if he was going to make a criticism. Which it appeared he was about to.

He followed Ben into the office, and Ben shut the door behind them. The wide windows in the space had the best view in the building, and the room had been tastefully decorated in neutral shades.

Ben gestured toward the leather couch. "Have a seat."

Cameron sat. Ben went around to the other side of his desk and sank into the wingback chair. He rested his elbows on the desk, steepling his fingers in front of him.

"So. While you were gone, I was reviewing some of our security camera footage from last month. I don't normally do that, but everyone told me someone had shoveled the snow around the clinic during all those storms we got in February, while I was out of town. I wanted to thank whoever it was."

Cameron leaned forward. "Who *was* doing all the shoveling? I never found out."

"Vanessa's boyfriend. Turns out he was worried about her slipping in those heeled boots."

"She does wear ridiculous heels."

"Her prerogative." Ben waved a dismissive hand. "But I also saw something else. You. Coming and going from the clinic at all hours. You were supposed to be off for a week while I was gone."

Cameron's stomach dropped another few notches. This was exactly what he'd hoped to keep hidden from Ben. Vanessa had promised she wouldn't tell on him, but of course, Ben had found out anyway.

"I—"

Ben's expression hardened. "I meant what I said about staff taking their required time off. Why were you here working on your vacation time?"

Cameron swallowed. "I wasn't working on clinic business. It was schoolwork. My wifi at home is slow, and I'm more used to getting things done here."

Ben leaned forward. "So you worked all week, every day, until late at night. But you thought it was okay because it was work for school?"

"Kind of?"

"Because it feels a bit like you were sneaking around. I'm sure the only reason you didn't come in to work last week was because I was here and I'd have seen you."

Cameron slumped back on the couch. The thing about Ben was that he saw everything, noticed everything.

"I'm sorry." He pinched the bridge of his nose between his fingers. "I *was* coming in that week because I thought you wouldn't find out. That's on me. I was just... It's been really hard to—"

He broke off, swallowing hard around the sudden tightness in his throat. He would not have a breakdown in front of Ben. But apparently, opening the door to one emotion led to all kinds of other things pouring out.

He scrubbed a hand over his face, trying to pull himself together.

"Cameron." Ben's voice was gentle. "You're overworking yourself."

"I know that. I know. I admit that I have...a problem with working too much." He sucked in a breath, then another, until he got his voice back under control.

"But what can I do? Quit school? I'm too close to being done. But now I have to redo all the data from my study and rewrite a huge section of my dissertation."

"I can't advise you on your schoolwork. But you should talk to your supervisor about it."

Cameron snorted a laugh. "That won't work. He's the actual worst human being on the planet."

"Hmm." Ben leaned back in his chair, looking thoughtful. "There's only one other thing I can think of to help you out."

"What's that?"

"Put you on leave."

Cameron shot up straight on the couch, panic threading through his veins. "No. Don't do that."

"I don't want to do it. But maybe, if you were forced to take a break—"

"Please don't. I can make it all work, and I won't sneak in

157

after hours again. I promise."

Thank God Ben hadn't found out about his disastrous meeting with Sasha, the night he'd fallen asleep at Matt's desk. That would be one more strike against him at this point.

Ben studied him for a long moment. "I honestly don't know what the best thing to do is in this situation. But I'm serious about your mental health."

"I know you are."

"I mean it, Cameron. If you stay on here, you have to show me you'll be able to function. I won't have you working yourself to death on my watch. That's not who we are."

"I know. The clinic is so good about things like that. I'd hoped, after I graduated, things might slow down. And you said there's a new position opening up on staff. You know I want it, so I have to graduate on time this spring."

Ben regarded him with a serious expression. "And I want you on the team as a therapist. But I need to know you can take care of yourself, too. It doesn't work to take care of others and not yourself. Believe me, I've tried it."

"I can take care of myself. At least, I'm working on learning how."

But the truth was, maybe he couldn't take care of himself, couldn't see the limits of his own capabilities. He'd spent seven years proving that fact, driving himself too hard. He'd been as reckless as Robbie in his own way, burning through his reserves without a care.

Ben tilted his head to the side, considering. "Okay. I won't put you on leave. But I want you to update me on how your semester is going. Once a week. We'll check in and see how you're doing. If you need a break—"

"I won't—"

"If we both decide together that a break might be a good idea, it will not threaten your future here at the clinic, understand? You'll be able to come back. But this is your health we're talking about."

"I understand."

"Good. Well, I can tell I've embarrassed you. You can go back out front now. But make sure you take lunch today."

"Of course." It was embarrassing, the way his boss felt like he had to remind him to eat, like a child.

He closed Ben's office door behind him on his way out. Back at his desk, he clicked and sorted the emails in his inbox on autopilot, his brain racing.

Everyone in his life could see how burnt out he was. He'd thought he was better at hiding it, but first Sasha, and now Ben, had seen right through him.

He couldn't be a good therapist in this state. And even though Ben had said he wouldn't lose his job, he'd also made it clear he expected different behavior from his employees.

Cameron had admitted he had a problem. And putting it out there in the open had threatened the foundations of every one of his plans.

All he had was his work, and if he didn't have that, he no longer knew who he was. And he could think of only one person he wanted to talk to about it, one person who might understand what it felt like to have your future feel uncertain, threatened.

He reached for his phone, but there were no new messages from Sasha. However soon was too soon to text your friend with benefits, he was probably about to cross that line.

Chapter 16

On Tuesday afternoon, Sasha paused mid-workout, swiped her forehead with a towel, and checked her phone screen. Normally, she ignored the device while working out. But Cameron had been quiet for two days, and she'd checked her messages a ridiculous number of times.

She never waited on texts from a man. But she and Cameron had parted on strange terms Saturday night. Unlike every other guy she'd known, he hadn't seemed all that thrilled with the idea of regular, no-strings sex. She couldn't seem to wipe from her memory the expression on his face, sad and conflicted rather than relieved he'd been offered an out.

She'd told herself she shouldn't sleep with him too many times in a row, because continuing to sleep with someone was how things got too messy, too close to what some people might call a relationship. She'd already admitted they were friends, which was bad enough. Dating was not for someone like her, someone who'd been burned by unreliable men one too many times.

After they'd said goodbye, she'd half expected not to hear back from Cameron again. Which absolutely did not make her feel any type of way. But he wouldn't ghost her.

Cameron was a good guy. One who probably wanted a steady girlfriend. Someone he could see himself being with long-term. He'd said as much the other night, when he said he wasn't sure he could do casual.

He wouldn't want anything serious with her, though. That privilege would be reserved for a woman without as much of a past as she had. The perfect woman for Cameron was a college graduate with a steady office job and a nice business casual wardrobe. Not someone with a probation officer.

She jabbed at the punching bag a little too hard, then ducked out of the way as it whistled by too close to her head. Another woman wouldn't understand him the way she did. Another woman wouldn't see the ways he pushed himself too hard, and what buttons allowed him to relax and let go. He wouldn't have as much fun with another woman.

Anyway, she still had his camera. He'd need to come pick it up at some point. She'd given up on the workout, picked up her things, and headed to the showers when her phone buzzed with a text.

Cameron: Do you want to get together? Maybe tonight?

A thrill shot through her, and she fought to keep from smiling at her phone in the middle of the crowded gym. She had no reason to be happy about a simple text, but there it was.

Sasha: I could be persuaded.

Cameron: Would you want to maybe come to my place after work? I can show you my comic collection.

Sasha: That sounds like a pickup line.

Cameron: Is it working?

Sasha: I think it might be. 7:00? I can bring the memory card to check?

Cameron: See you then.

He texted her his address, and she opened her maps app, surprised to find they only lived about ten minutes apart from one another. She'd have thought Cameron might live in a more expensive part of town, but grad students didn't get paid much. She'd also assumed his family would help him out, but apparently they hadn't.

After her evening classes, she showered and changed, then headed to his place. An unusual sliver of nerves shot through her as she pulled into his parking lot and knocked on his door. She was about to be alone with him again, but not in a public place this time, and not at her place of work.

He'd invited her over to hook up, or he'd implied it. That had been their agreement the other night. Casual, no-strings fun.

But when he opened the door, thoughts of hooking up fled her mind. He looked exhausted again. The dark circles were back under his eyes, and even worse, his expression had that flat look she'd noticed the night they'd met. Like he wasn't all there.

"What's wrong?" she asked, stepping inside and inspecting his face.

"What do you mean?"

"I mean, you look terrible."

A smile turned up the corner of his mouth, but it didn't reach his eyes. "I've been hearing that a lot, from a lot of people. It's nothing. Just had a stressful day at work."

"That's all you're going to tell me?"

He gave a short nod. "For now. I'm honestly tired of thinking about it."

"Okay. For now." She had time to figure out what was going on with him.

She scanned the small apartment as they stepped inside, and wasn't surprised the space was neat and spare. A dark blue couch and recliner faced a small TV screen in the living room area, and the dining area held a dark wooden table and two chairs, open to a tiny kitchen. Neatly stacked crates of comic books sat on the coffee table, alongside a notebook, pens, and a laptop. He hadn't put much up on the walls, but a set of bookshelves on the far wall displayed a healthy-sized book collection.

"Do you want to sit?" he asked. "We can check the memory card first, if you like." He gestured her toward the couch, and she sat on the edge of it, not removing her jacket.

Here in his own space, he seemed more like the Cameron she'd met a few weeks ago—quiet and sober. Like a weight was on him. He'd been back at work for two days after spring break, and already he looked like this again. No sign of the funny, sweet guy who'd let himself fall apart with her the other day.

Wordlessly, she pulled the memory card from her pocket

and handed it to him. He opened the laptop and inserted the disk. While he waited for it to load, he slid a glance her way.

"Sorry. I didn't offer you anything to drink."

"I'm fine. I appreciate you letting us keep using the camera."

"Not a problem."

God, they sounded like a couple of strangers. Someone would have to break the ice.

"I can scan through the footage from the night hours first?" he offered.

"Okay."

She watched as he scrubbed through the video. At a sudden flicker on the screen, he stopped the playback.

"What are you looking at?" she asked, peering over his shoulder.

"There were people walking by. Uh, the other night, when we were…"

"Occupied?" she suggested.

A tiny smile curved his mouth, this one looking a touch more genuine. "Yeah. That."

"Let's start there, then."

Cameron set the playback so the video ran at triple speed, people appearing and disappearing quickly in the camera's field as the evening went on.

"Wait." She reached out and hit the spacebar. A bolt of white-hot fury lanced through her. "Son of a bitch."

"Is that them?" he asked.

"Yeah. It's them."

The grainy black and white video showed three young men in jeans and oversized jackets, strolling around the square. To an observer, they might look like teenagers out having fun.

"Which one of them…" Cameron's hand had curled into a

fist on his thigh.

She swallowed. "The tallest one. On the left."

Cameron turned to her, his eyes widening. "You fought *that* one?"

"That's the guy." She tried to make her voice sound casual, but her heart raced at the sight of his square jaw, blond crew cut, and smallish, narrow eyes. He'd been right there, right across the square from the truck, while she and Cameron…

She jumped up from the couch and paced the room to the far wall, then back to the couch where Cameron waited for her, looking up at her with a dawning understanding.

"You're mad we missed them."

"Damn right."

"But they didn't do anything that night. They were just walking around. No one reported any damage."

"If I'd seen them, I could have called the police. Done something."

"But now we have footage proving they're back, scoping the neighborhood out. We have a face."

"I hate that guy's face," she grumbled, dropping onto the couch next to him.

Cameron stayed silent for a moment before speaking again. "Sasha. That guy is huge."

"Yeah. And?"

She knew what he was getting at. Maybe it *had* been unwise to take on a two-hundred-pound, angry, racist asshole by herself. At the time, she'd had adrenaline on her side.

She looked over to find Cameron's eyes on her with a strange intensity. "And I don't like thinking about you anywhere near him. So I'm glad we missed them."

So Cameron was a tiny bit protective of her. Which was not

at all attractive. She could take care of herself, as she'd already proven.

"I hate waiting around for them to show up again," she said. "If I'd known they were there... But I let myself get distracted."

There was a long pause. She looked across the couch to find Cameron rubbing the back of his neck, looking uncomfortable.

"Are you sorry about what happened the other night?"

His expression was hard to read. He looked so tired, and sort of defeated, and she had the unfamiliar urge to wrap him in a hug.

With any other guy, this would be the point where she called things off, because it was getting too complicated. Because it wasn't good for her focus or his. But she couldn't bring herself to say the words.

"No. I'm not sorry," she said after a minute.

"I'm...not sorry, either. And I'll keep helping you figure this out. You can keep the camera as long as you need it. You'll get more footage next time they come, which will also be proof they've come more than once. I know you're mad things are taking so long, but we're getting closer to catching them. And in the meantime, I can volunteer on weekends, if your dad needs the help."

Somewhere in the middle of his speech, her mouth had dropped open, pulse picking up in her chest. Not many people offered to help her, free and clear of them getting anything in return.

"Why are you being so nice to me?" The words came out before she could stop them, sounding a hell of a lot more vulnerable than she'd intended. "Because we're...friends?"

He shook his head, shutting his eyes for a moment before fixing them on her.

"Saturday night meant something to me. If all we are is friends, I'd still want to help you. But I care about you, probably more than a friend should. Maybe that's not what you want to hear. I tried not to. I don't know how it happened, but it did. But don't worry, I won't put any pressure on you for more, because I know that's not what you want."

She drew in a shaky inhale, then another. A riot of feelings bloomed in her chest, and surprisingly, none of them made her want to run in the opposite direction.

"Cameron. I'm going to hug you now. If that's okay with you."

"I could use it, honestly."

She slid closer to him on the couch, opened her arms, and drew him into them. He was so much taller than her, he had to bend his head to lay it on her shoulder. He felt good in her arms, right, and her body loosened, like she could take a deep breath for the first time since she'd left him the other night.

This didn't have to mean anything. Anything other than being friends who cared about each other. Cared maybe more than friends typically did.

She rested her chin on his head, smelling his warm, lived-in aftershave.

"So," she said. "Are you still going to show me your comic collection?"

* * *

An hour later, they'd spread out the comics around them on the couch. She'd convinced him to read her one of his favorites,

167

and she'd scooted back against the arm of the couch with him reclining between her knees, his back to her front. Cameron lay pillowed on her chest, holding the comic in front of them as he read aloud.

She'd shrugged off her jacket and looped her arms around his shoulders, playing her fingers over his chest while his deep voice impersonated all the characters. The story was interesting, about an alien planet where humans went to take vacations. She could get used to reading more comics like this.

She'd gotten distracted at several points during the story, rubbing his shoulders and feeling his muscles soften under her hands.

He paused his reading. "You're trying to make me fall asleep again. This is your secret mission in life."

"Nope. I think I like the relaxed version of you better."

He laid the comic book down on his lap. "I'm sorry if I seemed stressed out earlier."

She smoothed a hand over his hair, the curls soft and springy under her fingers.

"So something happened at work."

"Yeah. My boss threatened to put me on leave if I didn't stop working late. Causing me to question everything about myself. Then after that, my... The woman I'm seeing beat up some guy who, it turns out, is the size of an actual yeti."

A laugh burst out of her. "You really don't like that idea."

He shook his head. "I can't stand thinking about it. I saw enough of that growing up. Like I told you, my brother got into a lot of fights."

"And you were the peacemaker."

"Not so much the peacemaker. More like, he left a lot of messes in his wake, and someone had to be the responsible one, the one who cleaned everything up. My dad worked all the time, and Mom couldn't deal with it alone after a certain point. Some days, she was so stressed, she couldn't get out of bed."

"So you had to step up."

He nodded. "Yep. I'd cook dinner, clean the house, whatever needed to be done that day. I guess I had to be a grownup pretty young. Hyper-competence, some people call it."

"This is all making way too much sense. You were a little adult as a kid. And you're still that way."

"Except I'm an actual adult now."

"One who works too much. I don't want you to end up like your mom."

He paused for a long moment before answering. "Me neither."

"So I'm glad you have your comics back. Something just for fun."

"Fun is good."

"I know some other fun things, too." She trailed her hand suggestively down his torso. He captured her wrist and pressed a kiss to the inside of it, before turning his head to face her. His expression was softer, easier now than it had been since she'd walked in the door. She'd done that for him, helped him find his calm place again.

Their mouths were inches apart, but he didn't kiss her, and even though everything in her ached to press her mouth to his, she waited for him to make the first move.

She searched his face. Why wasn't she tired of him yet? Usually by this point, she'd had more than her fill of any one man.

He removed his glasses and set them on the coffee table, on

top of the comic. He twisted his torso until he faced her and placed a hand on the side of her face, looking into her eyes.

"This is more than just fun for me," he said.

Her heart beat a wild rhythm in her chest, but no words came out of her mouth. He'd always been a serious guy, but now, with all that serious attention focused on her, her attraction to him exploded into a new level of awareness.

He was the hottest thing she'd ever seen, all intense eyes and flushed cheeks, studying her like she was the most interesting thing in his world.

Her fingertips tingled, and heat bloomed in her chest, up her neck. Her hand shook slightly as she lifted it and touched his lips.

"Are you ever going to kiss me?" she asked.

"I am. And then...I'm going to do some things I didn't get to do the other night."

"Okay." Why couldn't she catch her breath?

His mouth came down on hers, stealing any further thoughts. It was even better than last time, sweeter, because he moved slower than she did, exploring her mouth and trailing kisses down her neck.

Her head fell back on the cushion as he rolled on top of her, his weight warm and hard against her. She'd never been the biggest fan of having a guy on top of her. It was too vulnerable, too open. But she'd try it with him, because she trusted him. He wouldn't hurt her or take advantage of the position to make it all about him.

He was, in fact, doing everything he could to drive her out of her mind. He explored every inch of her skin, but he was moving too slowly, spreading heat everywhere he touched.

He pushed up her shirt and kissed her breasts until she was

panting and shaky, then made her come twice with his mouth and fingers. By the time he rolled on a condom and pushed inside her, she was impossibly spiraling up for one more round.

He moved over her, and she matched his rhythm, a perfect pairing of urgency and sweetness. He took care with her, touching her as if she was precious, as if she meant something to him, and she let herself try on the feeling. Imagine it might be real. A third orgasm wrenched through her, and this time, Cameron came with her, gasping her name.

Afterward, he rolled to the side and pillowed his head on her arm. Idly, his hand stroked over the tattoo on her hip. She rolled her too-heavy head to look down at him.

"That's my Aries constellation."

"I thought so." His fingers traced the line of stars, then traveled over to explore the ink on her arms. "So… are Aries and Aquarius a good match?"

"Yeah. They're good. As long as no one tries to tell Aries what to do."

"Got it."

"I thought you didn't believe in astrology."

"Well, I guess if I can believe in space travel and aliens, why not stars?" His hand smoothed over her hip and belly. "These are so beautiful. You're beautiful."

People had told her that before, and she'd never felt like they meant it on anything but a superficial level. But it was different coming from him. She pressed a soft kiss to his forehead.

"You're feeling okay?" he asked.

"I've been practicing naming my feelings, you know. In therapy."

"I do know."

"And I'm feeling…pretty happy right now."

She rolled the word around in her mind, but it fit. Improbably, being with this man made her happy. If they could have more days together, she'd take them.

He still hadn't asked her to be anything other than friends with benefits, but his feelings were there in every touch, every word he gave her.

At some point, he was going to ask her for more. And she didn't know what she'd say when he did.

Chapter 17

Ten days later, Cameron whistled as he shut the car door and jogged across the square to pick up Sasha. Sasha, who he'd spent three of the last ten evenings with. She'd come over to his apartment after work twice, and once, she'd even let him pick her up from the gym.

That night, she'd spent the night in his bed for the first time, leaving him dizzy with happiness. This didn't feel like friends.

They weren't calling it dating. They weren't calling it anything at all. But she'd stopped asking if she'd see him again when they said goodbye, because she knew she would.

He'd made slow progress reconstructing some of the charts for his study. He wasn't working fast enough to get it done on time, but every night, he shut down his laptop at 5:00 and stopped working anyway.

Every night, the work stopped, and some nights, he got to have this. Her opening the door to the food truck and waving at him, the wide smile on her face making his heart jump in his chest. He hurried toward her, and away from his schoolwork.

He would ask her tonight how she felt. Ten days was a long time. She could have changed her mind about the whole no-relationships thing. He could tell her he'd changed his own mind on the subject. There was no point in saying he had no room in his life for a relationship, that his life was too full with school and work, when he'd ditched school at every opportunity to see her.

They had the spark of something growing between them. She had to see that by now.

"Hello." She dropped a kiss onto his mouth when he reached her, from her position on the truck steps. "I'm almost ready. I have one more tray to wash."

"You can leave it." Alexei's voice carried out of the truck from behind her. "I'll get it. Go have fun."

"You're sure?" she asked.

Alexei's broad shoulders appeared in the door frame behind her. "I'm sure. I do this every day for how many decades, and you think I can't handle it?"

"I didn't say that." She rolled her eyes, facing Cameron so Alexei couldn't catch the expression. "I stopped by after my classes to put in some extra hours, but he got grumpy about it."

"That's because I can do it on my own," Alexei said. He shot an exasperated look at Cameron. "But you can't stop Sasha when she gets an idea of what she wants to do. I don't know where she got that from."

"No idea," Cameron said, keeping a straight expression.

He'd been nervous about meeting Sasha's father last week, but Alexei hadn't been nearly as intimidating as he appeared. Like his daughter, he had a hard shell, but that was only part of the picture.

He'd thanked Cameron several times for lending them the camera, speculating that maybe the vandals had seen it, and it had scared them off from doing any further damage. The square had been quiet for two weeks now, and Alexei thought maybe it was all over now. They'd decided to keep the cameras recording longer, just to be safe.

Sasha had told him her dad seemed relieved, some of the strain of worry off his shoulders. She'd hugged him for the longest time after she'd told him that.

Another fact to add to his growing pile of evidence that this was more than friendship. He'd lined up careful arguments he could use to persuade her. But it would be tricky.

Much as she'd tease him for over-analyzing things, he'd thought it through. He could present it to her as a series of steps. From casual dating to something more. It wouldn't have to be a giant leap into a committed relationship, something that would probably send her running in the opposite direction.

But dating was trickier than data analysis. The feelings slipped out from under his fingers when he tried to pin them down. And his emotions had the tendency to balloon dangerously when he was around her.

When they got into his car, he handed her the small bunch of spring violets he'd bought on the way here. She took them, a strange expression on her face.

"What is it?" he asked. "Maybe you're not the flowers type..."

She shook her head. "You wouldn't know. They were my mom's favorite flower. Her name was Sigal. It means 'violet.'" She held out her wrist, gesturing to her mother's name tattoo, the ink bracelet around her wrist.

"I'm sorry. I didn't mean to make you sad."

"You didn't. I like them. I don't remember Mom, almost at

all. But Dad talked about her all the time when I was growing up. Like she was always there with him, as real as if she was still alive, or like she'd passed a month ago, rather than years."

Cameron swallowed. "He really loved her."

"He still does. Like no time has passed. I think that's a big reason why I got the tattoo. Almost more to remind myself of Dad's love, if that makes any sense." She paused, thinking for a moment. "I guess, when you love someone like that, they're with you forever. That was what my parents had, at least."

Cameron's hands tightened on the steering wheel. Even though she claimed to only want a casual relationship, there was a part of her that did believe in love. She just didn't seem to believe it was for her.

He should tell her now. That he had feelings. That he couldn't see her as a friend anymore. But the right words evaded him. He couldn't talk about his feelings now, not with the soft memories of her parents' love floating between them.

Could he call his feelings for her love? They'd stolen over him, covered him with a blanket of rightness when he was with her. His feelings were confusing as hell. But he'd heard love was like that.

The evening breeze stirred her glossy hair, casting her bright, inked skin with a warm glow. Her curves, her strength, the way she was angry and joyful and defiant all at once—she was more than the sum of her parts. An equation he'd be happy to study for the foreseeable future.

"So, where are we headed tonight?" she asked.

He cleared his throat. "If you're up for it, I thought I could take you to the rare bookstore? They're open late on Fridays."

"This is your comic place?"

"Yeah."

"Then yes, I want to see it. Then you're going to feed me something that is not a knish. I can only take so many of them."

He laughed. "Got it."

"Then we could go for a drive? The flowering trees are all blooming. If we take the parkway downtown, we can see them all with the windows down."

"Sounds like a plan."

He'd tell her later, on their drive, and maybe he'd get to hold the flame of her in his hand a little bit longer.

When they entered the bookstore, Luka took one look at Sasha and launched into a torrent of Ukrainian.

Laughing, Sasha held up a hand. "I can't understand… It's too fast. But yeah, I'm Alexei's daughter."

Cameron stared at her. "It's a small world."

She raised a brow at him. "Definitely among the Ukrainian community here. Luka and my dad know each other from the community center. But we haven't seen each other since I was, what? Fifteen?"

She turned to Luka for confirmation, and the older man gave a nod.

"Your dad said you grew up too fast," Luka said. "He told me you've been teaching self-defense classes?"

"I have. At a fitness center."

"That's good. And you managed to find a nice boy, too." He raised an eyebrow, tilting his head in Cameron's direction. His tone lifted at the end of the sentence, making it into a partial question. Sasha outranked him in Luka's affections, which was fine.

"He's… Yeah, I guess I did."

Luka turned to Cameron, fixing him with a stern expression. "You be very good to this one. Or you can't buy my comics anymore."

"Of course."

Luka gave a nod. "I'll let you shop, then."

After the older man had stepped into the other room, Cameron turned to Sasha.

"I thought Luka was my friend. But apparently you're more important."

She smiled up at him. "Obviously, I'm more important."

"Look, I know he assumed we're dating—"

"It's fine. We don't have to explain everything to him. Show me around. I knew Dad's friend had a bookstore, but I didn't know this was the one."

He showed her the used and rare book sections, the comics, and the vintage sci-fi collection. Luka brought out a bin of old martial arts movie tie-in books from the 1970s, and they went to the corner armchair to explore. Sasha plopped onto his lap with a stack of books, and a bubble of lightness swelled in his chest, making it difficult to concentrate on reading.

Her casual ownership of his space felt right. She should sit on his lap, or pet his hair, like she'd done when they'd read together on his couch. He wouldn't have recognized the person in this chair a month ago.

After she'd been absorbed in the martial arts books for an hour, he bought her a few to start her own collection. He pictured them organizing their book collections together in the future, which was taking things ten steps too far.

One step at a time was smarter. But it wasn't what he'd want, if he could have anything. For once, the smarter choice didn't appeal. But life never handed you good things without hard work, and he was good at working towards a goal.

At dinner, they sat next to each other in a corner booth at a

Mediterranean bistro that served tapas and wine. Sasha didn't drink much, but she put away her share of food. After the meal, she leaned back in the booth, patting her stomach.

"That was perfect," she said.

"Sure you don't want the tiramisu?"

She raised a brow at him. "Want it? Yes. But I don't think it will fit in my stomach at this point. Some other time, though."

"We could order it, and you could have a couple of bites. You don't have to finish it." Whatever she wanted, he wanted to give it to her. In whatever form.

She leaned her elbows on the table, her eyes twinkling. "If I didn't know you better, I'd say you're trying to spoil me. Ordering a dessert and not eating it is very impractical. So unlike you."

"Then I guess I'm not always practical."

She studied him for a moment. "No, you're not, are you? If you were, you'd—"

She broke off, looking away quickly.

"I'd what?"

"It's nothing."

"Tell me." He leaned forward, put a hand on her forearm. Her skin was warm to the touch, and he couldn't help stroking his fingers over the softness, the colors of her ink.

She brought her gaze back to his, her expression conflicted.

"It's just... Wouldn't you rather find a real girlfriend? I mean, I know you said you don't do casual. Don't you want to find someone you could be with long term? Someone more...like-minded?" The side of her mouth twisted downward on the last word, as if it tasted bad.

He sat back, stunned into silence, his brain churning. Did she really think he could want someone other than her at this point? Was she saying she didn't want to be the one for him? Or maybe she didn't have the self-confidence or the belief she could be the one.

She was the most confident person he'd ever met, in some areas. And in others, she seemed completely unsure of herself.

"I did say, at the start, that I wasn't sure a no-strings thing would work for me," he said slowly. "Are you saying you still don't want a relationship?"

He leaned forward, holding her gaze. "Or are you saying you don't think I'd want to be with *you*? Because if that's what you think—"

She shifted her gaze away. "That is what I think sometimes. I can't help it. I've really… I like seeing you. It's a lot better than one-night stands, and I never realized it could be like that. At least not for me."

"So you've only ever done random hookups. Once with the same guy, and that's it?"

She lifted a shoulder. "Sometimes twice. But yeah. It was easier to keep things casual."

"But not with me." He couldn't keep the intensity out of his voice. "We've spent three weeks together, and not all of it in bed."

She gave a short nod, but she didn't look happy about it.

"Sasha, you have to know—"

"Don't. Don't say anything else. I ruined our night by saying what I did. Can we forget the last five minutes just happened?"

"Why? Tell me what's wrong."

Five minutes ago, she'd looked happy, almost glowing. Now her expression had shuttered. His gut clenched, all his plans of declaring his feelings scrapped, because she'd told him she didn't want to hear it.

She didn't want him. Or she thought he wouldn't want someone like her, which was the most outrageous part of all.

It was so obvious now, in retrospect. Her repeated questions about her background, her record, and why it didn't bother him. Her past issues with being treated like dirt by men, especially men in authority. She'd never let a man in, because that way, she'd never have a chance to be hurt by one, either.

He wanted no woman but her. No one else had ever made him feel anything until she'd blasted him open. But she didn't want to hear about it.

"Can we go on that drive now? Or you can take me home, if you want." She raised her hand for the check, sounding almost desperate.

She wouldn't meet his eyes. She wanted to get away from the unspoken conversation between them.

"Yeah." The word was a stone falling from his mouth. "We can go."

Chapter 18

T he night air was warm, pouring through the open windows of Cameron's car, and Sasha stuck her hand out, feeling the breeze playing over her fingers. Cameron had been quiet as he'd steered them toward downtown, and as they turned onto the winding parkway that would take them by the river, she turned her face away from him so he wouldn't see her expression.

She'd been close to saying something, back at the restaurant. Close to admitting she cared about him. She'd never been good at mild emotions. It was all or nothing, and somehow, over the last few weeks, she'd gotten attached to Cameron.

But that didn't mean a relationship could work for them in the long run. Caring about someone didn't mean you got to have them in your life. One more reason to keep things casual.

They were too different. He was about to earn his doctorate, and she was on probation. He had a brilliant future ahead, and all she had were family problems and legal troubles.

And even though he'd never judged her, he'd wake up one

day and realize he didn't want this. It was only a matter of time.

The heavy scent of flowering trees filled the car, and her heart thumped hard in her chest. It would be so easy to reach across the console and take his hand, tell him she did have feelings for him. He'd been about to say the same, back at the dinner table. Before she interrupted and told him not to.

She wanted him, more than she'd ever wanted to try with anyone else. She'd never been afraid of taking risks with her body. But her heart was another matter.

Maybe they could coast like this for a while longer. Not friends, and not dating either. From the devastated look on Cameron's face back at the restaurant, it might not be possible for him to keep this up, though.

She didn't want to lose him. She'd miss falling into bed with him. But she'd also miss laughing as they snuck around the square after dark. Cuddling in the armchair at the used bookstore.

He was too different from her, but also somehow her perfect complement. Frighteningly perfect.

"It's, uh… It's a really warm night," he said, breaking the silence.

"Yeah. Early spring. It'll be cold again in two days."

"Most likely."

They were awkward strangers all of a sudden, and she couldn't stand it. His posture was stiff, his voice formal. How she imagined him acting at work. No one else got to see the side of him she had, the side with the unconventional sense of humor and free-ranging mind.

She wanted that version of him back. But that Cameron had disappeared since dinner.

She swallowed. "I'm sorry about what I said back there."

He slanted her a look. "Are you?"

"I don't want to hurt you. And I don't want to stop seeing you," she said in a rush. "I just don't know if I can do anything more. I can't do relationships like other people can. Maybe that part of me is broken."

He steered the car around a sloping curve, under an archway of flowering trees. It should have been beautiful, breathtaking.

He was silent for a few long moments. "I guess I'll take casual, if casual is all you can offer. I can't stand… I'd rather have that than not see you at all."

"Okay." Her heart thrashed around in her chest in protest.

He drew in a deep inhale. "So we'll just…keep on like we have been."

His tone was light, but a world of hurt lay beneath the words.

She wanted to pull the emergency brake, climb into his lap, and yank him to her. Her heart thought he belonged to her, but she had to let go of that illusion. Her hands clenched into fists on her thighs.

"I thought it's been going pretty well so far," she said. "How we've been doing things."

The words sounded lame as soon as they were out. Not nearly enough.

"Yeah. Pretty well," he echoed.

They turned another corner, and the square came into view. Food trucks lined the edges, and streetlights lit the area, making it bright and cheerful. Happy people wandered around, holding hands, listening to the free live music.

"I can drop you back at your car," he offered, in that same light tone, the one he'd use on a stranger.

He'd brought her back early. Her car was parked a few blocks away, and he was leaving her now, no offer to come back to his place. This was what people did when things were casual between them.

"Okay." She gripped the door handle as if it would keep her anchored, kept her eyes plastered out the window.

A flash of movement on the south side of the square caught her eye. A shadow that shouldn't be there, slipping along the brick wall of a storefront. A big shadow of a man with a buzz cut. The hair on her arms stood up.

"Stop the car."

Cameron shot her a surprised look, but he pulled over. She was out the door the second he stopped, sprinting toward the motion. She heard footsteps behind her, the sound of Cameron following on her heels.

Her eyes tracked the movement of the shadow, the way it slipped around the street corner. She picked up her pace, legs pumping to get closer before the man escaped.

Her mind had emptied of everything but the one objective. Catch him. She'd figure out what to do next once he was in her sight again.

It was this man's fault her family and neighbors lived in fear. His fault that she was in legal trouble she didn't deserve. His fault that her life was the mess it had become. Her pounding feet punctuated the words in her mind.

She shot down a side alley, gaining on him. In a moment, he'd be close enough to see, close enough to... What? She didn't have a plan for when she got to him. Only that she wasn't going to lose him this time. He didn't get to run away again and get off free.

At the back of the alley, a tall wooden fence rattled as the man climbed it. She had an instant to see his face, to recognize

185

him, before he disappeared over the top of it.

She hurled herself at the fence, but it was too tall, and she scanned the space frantically for a foothold.

"Sasha, wait." Cameron appeared at the mouth of the alley, out of breath and bracing his hands on his knees. "What the hell are you doing?"

"Help me up. Give me a foothold so I can get over." She paced the end of the alley, adrenaline and nerves spiking in her bloodstream.

"What? No. No way. Do you even hear yourself right now?"

"He's getting away. Please, Cameron. Help me do this."

He shook his head. "I can't. I won't let you do that."

He looked shaken, his face pale as if he'd seen a ghost.

She rounded on him, her adrenaline transforming into rage. "You won't let me. You don't get to decide what I do."

"You're the only one who can decide."

"But you won't help me."

"Of course I won't help you hurt yourself." He said the words as if he was speaking to a small child, one who didn't understand the world. When she did understand.

What she understood was that the bad guy had gotten away again, and as usual, nothing was fair. Nothing was ever made right.

With a cry of frustration, she hurled a punch into the wooden fence, then immediately regretted it. Cradling her aching fist in her hand, she looked up in time to see Cameron take a step toward her.

"Stay away from me right now," she hurled at him. "You don't want to get anywhere close to me like this."

He flinched as if she'd hit him, instead of the wall.

"I can't help you do this," he said. "Because I care about you too much. You're worth too much to me. But if you can't believe that about yourself…"

He held up both hands in a gesture of surrender. "Maybe you're right. Maybe we don't belong together."

It was exactly what she'd suspected he'd say one day. She just hadn't expected that day to be today.

The words knocked the wind out of her. They hurt more than her bleeding fist.

"Then you'd better get going," she told him, her tone hard as steel. It came easier to act tough, like this didn't matter. Better he think she was hard and cold than see an inkling of what was going on beneath the surface.

Cameron looked at her for a long moment, as if memorizing her. He didn't look offended, or scared, or even put off by her temper rearing its head. Instead, he looked tired. Resigned.

He shut his eyes and shook his head, seeming to draw himself together. Then he turned and walked out of the alley without a backward glance. He walked stiffly, his shoulders set and his gaze straight ahead.

A good man, and a kind one. And she'd just proven without a doubt why they belonged in two different worlds.

* * *

By the time she'd jogged one block over to the square, a small group of people stood around the knish truck. She ran to the RV, heart in her throat. Glass shards surrounded the truck in a twenty-foot radius. The front two windows of the truck were gone, and one of the tires had been punctured.

Dad stood surveying the mess, hands on his hips.

"Dad! Are you okay?" she panted.

He spun to face her. "Sasha. What are you doing here?"

"We got back early. What happened?"

To her surprise, Dad threw back his head and laughed. Maybe he was in shock.

"Are you okay?" she asked.

"I'm fine," he reassured her, placing a large hand on her back. "I was washing the dishes in the back when I heard the crash. By the time I got to the door, they'd gone already. I'm glad you weren't here, though."

The old man kept smiling as he spoke.

"And you're happy about this because?"

"Because he got this." Anya stepped forward from the small group of people surrounding the truck, holding up the security camera. "We have a dozen witnesses and clear footage. This time, they won't get away with it."

The group surrounding the truck nodded and murmured their agreement.

"We're going to help Alexei clean up, as soon as the police take their report," Anya said.

"The police?" she echoed, feeling the blood rush from her face. Memories of her arrest flashed before her eyes, and she sank into a crouch before she blacked out.

"Don't worry." Dad stroked a hand over her hair. "You were nowhere near when it happened this time. We'll give them the footage and they'll take photos of the evidence. And will you let Cameron know? Thanks to him, we might be able to stop them for good this time."

"I'll tell him. I'm going to go inside and sit down for a minute."

Her voice sounded wooden to her own ears.

"Of course. Get a drink of water. You don't look so good." Dad narrowed his eyes at her. "Why were you running this way, anyway?"

"I just... I thought I saw someone. It set off my alarm bells."

"Hmph. Thank God you weren't around. If those men had found you, I wouldn't have been able to forgive myself. The truck doesn't matter, but you... You are irreplaceable."

She swallowed. "I know. People are the most important."

Inside the safety of the truck, she collapsed onto a chair, dropping her head into her hands. An unfamiliar combination of feelings swirled in her gut. Guilt that she hadn't been honest with Dad out there. Relief they'd gotten footage of the criminals, maybe even enough evidence to make a case to clear her record. Definitely enough evidence to prosecute.

Cameron had helped her by not lifting her over that fence. If she'd gone over it and confronted the criminals, she'd be in a new world of trouble right now. The police would question her, and she'd have a possible second offense on her record.

She'd teased Cameron when he'd gone on about "the power of information," but information was what would save them. Not hot-headed impulse.

She'd pushed him away, then gone running after a fight at the first chance.

"Why am I like this?" she asked the empty truck, but it didn't answer.

Outside, the flash of lights told her the police had arrived. It took over two hours for them to collect all the evidence they needed and interview witnesses, and Sasha spent the whole time hiding inside the truck.

She wasn't a witness. When they questioned her, she told

them she'd seen a shadow of a man running from the scene as she approached, which was the truth. And the extent of her involvement.

Then they were gone, and the community of food truck owners helped them clean up the broken glass and board over the windows. Everyone there had been helped by Alexei at some point, and they were happy to repay the favor.

In the morning, they'd call the insurance company about replacing the windows. She'd work extra hours to make sure Dad could meet the deductible.

When it was time to go home, Dad pulled her into a tight hug.

"Don't be sad about the truck, Sasha. I'm not. I'm only glad it's all over."

"Me too."

He pulled back to look at her, holding her at arm's length. "You're a good daughter. Your mom would be proud of you."

I'm not sure she would. Not with how I acted tonight.

She shook her head to clear it and fixed a smile on her face. "I think... She'd be proud of you, too."

Chapter 19

Cameron's research had shown him that everyone had a breaking point. Two weeks after breaking up with Sasha, he hit another level of no longer giving a fuck. After they'd parted that night, he'd gone home, pulled out his laptop, and plunged into his data analyses for the study. It was an easy habit to pick up again, his old friend the spreadsheet welcoming him back. Balance, he didn't know its name.

It was just like old times—pulling all-nighters, forgetting to eat. He was careful to leave work on time each day, though. Ben's watchful eye made sure he wasn't spending any extra hours at his desk. Because of that, he hadn't run into Sasha at any of her therapy appointments, because she met with Matt in the evenings.

But at home, he was a machine. Machines were lucky because they couldn't feel things. Couldn't suffer flashbacks of painful memories that made them pause and rub their eyes, as if they could erase the images that way.

She'd left her flowers on the seat of his car that night. He'd driven home with their sweet scent filling the car and her words in his ears.

You'd better get going.

As if he was a stranger, or worse, a threat to warn off. That had stung the most.

Well, that and the package he'd received at work a week later. Inside was the camera he'd lent her, carefully wrapped and addressed to him at The Well Space. A note inside from Alexei, thanking him for the device and telling him the memory card was with the police, as evidence.

His pulse had leapt at the news. Something had happened that night, either right before or right after he and Sasha arrived there. He'd combed the local papers for a story, but whatever had happened, it hadn't made the news.

Alexei would have mentioned if Sasha was hurt. She had to be okay, despite her reckless, wrongheaded instinct to go after the man who'd hurt her family.

So incredibly reckless. And also brave, and full of a fire he'd never possess. She'd been something that night, eyes blazing as she demanded he help her climb the wall.

And he'd frozen, every bad memory from his past rising up to keep him rooted in place. With the number of times he'd seen Robbie with bloody fists, it shouldn't have affected him so strongly. But he couldn't stand seeing her hurt. A wave of nausea had risen in his throat at the sight, and he'd fought it back.

She could choose to put herself in danger, with no regard for the value of her safety, but he could never do the same.

He'd done the right thing. But it had cost him the thing that meant the most in the world to him.

She'd only wanted casual dating anyway, something he

couldn't have kept up for much longer after that night. She'd told him upfront, "I use men for sex," and there was nothing wrong with her doing that. She just hadn't ever wanted anything more from him.

He'd been the deluded one who'd thought he could convince her otherwise.

After two weeks of killing himself with schoolwork, he woke up and realized he would not finish this study on time. It would have to be pushed back, and along with it, his graduation date. And possibly his dream job, out the window.

He'd emailed Dr. Gold at 8:00 a.m., when the man no doubt was still in bed, to tell him as much. And now he stood in front of his advisor's office door, ready to have the conversation he'd avoided and put off. The conversation where he gave up.

Up until recently, he'd have said this would be the worst conversation of his life. But that spot had been overtaken by the night he'd left Sasha.

He didn't knock on Dr. Gold's door, because he was done with all of it—manners, politeness, pretending he cared what the other man thought.

When the door swung open, it took his brain a moment to compute the image in front of him. Dr. Gold sat at his desk, head in his hands. His head jerked up at the noise, his eyes reddened, and his hair standing up as if he'd been running his hands through it.

He cleared his throat and smoothed a hand over his hair. "Cameron. I didn't hear you knock."

"I didn't. Are you all right?" His mind was still processing the fact that his advisor appeared to have been crying. Despite the fact that Gold was the biggest asshole on the planet, he might still be a human being.

"I'm fine." He cleared his throat again. "I had some...bad news this morning."

"I'm sorry to hear it. Did you get my email?"

"I did. Yes, of course." Gold looked around the room as if he didn't remember where he was. This was not the time to have an in-depth discussion about the data sets.

"I'll come back another time. I wanted to make sure the delay is okay with you, since you didn't reply to my message. We can push the due date back to October, right?"

"October. Yes, that'll be... That's fine."

He'd walked in here expecting sarcasm, a belittling tone. At least a mean-spirited joke about his lack of performance. Or the fact that he was now going to graduate a semester late.

Easy agreement, he hadn't expected.

"Cameron. I might be taking a leave of absence soon. I'll transfer you to another advisor within the department. Dr. Perkins. I think you'll get along well."

"Oh. Uh, thank you."

"She'll be able to find you some assistants too, I'm sure." Gold shook his head, a rueful expression on his face. "I haven't been all that helpful to you, have I? This has been a hard year for me, for...personal reasons. But that's not an excuse."

"It's okay," Cameron offered. The man's half-apology didn't make up for the hellish year of this study, but at least he seemed to have gained some self-awareness.

"Well. I'll email you when I know for sure," Gold said, gazing out the window.

"Okay, then. I hope you, uh. Take care."

His advisor hardly seemed to notice him leaving. Cameron backed out the door and shut it behind him.

Just like that, he had six more months of breathing room.

He'd clung so fiercely to the timeline of graduating in May, finishing the study by April. But in the end, no one cared in the slightest that it was happening late.

He drove to work and sat in the parking lot of The Well Space, staring out his windshield for a few minutes before going inside. Next up, his conversation with Ben. The one where he told Ben he wouldn't be done with school on time. The one where Ben would probably bring up putting him on leave again, and would definitely not consider him for the job on staff here.

Dreams were hard to give up on. Especially the one he'd worked the hardest for. But as it turned out, hard work wasn't enough sometimes.

He did knock on Ben's door, because he'd learned his lesson about knocking for the morning. And also because he respected Ben more than his advisor.

"Cameron. Come on in. Have a seat." Ben gestured to his couch, and Cameron sat on the edge of it. He'd gone over the words in his head before coming, but it didn't make them easier to say.

"I have to admit I was curious when you told me you had big news." Ben leaned forward in his chair, resting his elbows on his desk. "Good news, I hope?"

"Not exactly." Cameron sucked in a breath. "I've had to make a hard decision. I'm graduating late, because I couldn't finish my study on time. I'll submit the final dissertation in October, and I'll graduate in December, rather than May. I know this means you might hire someone else for the new position in the meantime—"

"Hold on." Ben held up a hand to stop him. "First of all, can you tell me what led you to postpone your study? I know you were juggling a lot of work the last time we talked."

"It was too much to get done by mid-April. No human being could have gotten through the workload. You're not going to like this, but I've spent the last two weeks trying my best not to sleep or eat, and it didn't matter. I woke up this morning and realized I couldn't do it. I failed."

"Hmm." Ben steepled his fingers in front of his chin. "Can I reframe that for you?"

"Go ahead and try."

"I know you pretty well, and I don't see this as a failure. In fact… I'm kind of pleased for you."

"Pleased," he echoed.

"Yes. The Cameron I knew the last year or so would have pushed himself to complete exhaustion. But you chose not to do that. You chose to stop and respect your limits. I see this as a positive change for you."

Cameron sat back on the couch. Of course, Ben had a point. The old Cameron would have died before quitting.

"The damned study is all about the effects of workplace stress," he grumbled.

Ben's eyes twinkled. "The irony of that wasn't lost on me."

"And I did everything I could to prove I was immune to stress. Other people gave in to it, but not me. But as it turns out, I'm as bad as anyone else."

"Or as good. What changed for you? I'm curious what made you rethink things."

"I… It's complicated."

He knew Ben well enough to talk about work or school, but they'd never discussed their private lives all that much. How to sum up the last month, from the moment he'd fallen asleep at Matt's desk to the moment he'd said goodbye to Sasha in a dark alley and walked away from her forever?

Ben stayed silent, letting him process.

"I guess I realized I wasn't having any fun with my work," he said. "And I think what saves people from the stress and pressure must be whatever brings them joy."

"You found something that makes you feel that way."

He swallowed. "I did. For a little while, anyway."

Ben tilted his head to one side. "And once you feel that, you can't go back to not feeling it anymore."

"That's right. I tried to fit myself back into the box I used to live in, and I couldn't do it. I slept late this morning. I even ate breakfast."

Ben smiled at him. "I'm glad to hear it. To your earlier point, I think you'll complete your study just fine. Because you've given yourself space to breathe, and maybe find that spark of what you loved about the work in the first place. You could even include your own experiences with work-related stress as a personal anecdote in your introduction."

"That's...not a bad idea."

"And as for what you said about us hiring someone else in the meantime..."

Cameron's hands clenched into fists on his thighs. Letting go of this would be hard. Second only to letting go of Sasha.

Ben leaned forward, as if imparting a confidential secret. "That position was created for you. It's yours, whenever you graduate. We'll be waiting to welcome you onto the therapy staff."

Cameron blinked, unable to say anything.

Ben leaned back in his chair. "Besides, Vanessa would kill me if I even considered opening up that job for outside applications. You've always been her favorite."

"Thank you." The words came out rough with emotion. "I don't know how I got so lucky."

"We'll be the lucky ones to have you on staff. And in the meantime, you should keep going after the things that bring you joy. It hasn't led you astray so far."

"I will. And thank you again."

He shut Ben's door behind him and made his way back to his desk. After booting up his laptop, he stared at the scheduling software he'd spent thousands of hours working in.

What could take ordinary work and make it a joy, rather than a burden? He'd had more fun chopping onions with Sasha than he'd had at work in the last few years.

He'd always liked working hard, but what gave the work meaning was connecting to other people. He'd gone into this field to help people, not just create spreadsheets. His brain was a tool to use, but that was his purpose, the engine that drove him.

Sasha had reminded him that joy existed. She'd been his friend first, then much more.

He shouldn't have left her alone in that alley, even if all she wanted from him was friendship. He could have stayed and talked her down. Walked with her to her family to check on them. Instead, he'd walked away.

He wanted to smack his own forehead. Just because he didn't want to help Sasha get into a fight was no reason to abandon her. It would have been hard to stay, hard to withstand the heat of her anger. But he could have done it for her.

He could have been a better friend to her in that moment. But he'd been too caught up in his own feelings, in what he'd wanted to get out of the situation. He hadn't seen what she needed.

Sasha had told him she didn't think she could be the right woman for him. Insecurity hovered beneath her tough surface, and he'd proved her fears right by leaving her there. By walking away, he'd shown her that what she expected from men was true.

Maybe, if he'd stayed, they could have grown closer from the experience. He'd never know now.

He had a lot to learn about relationships. But he'd never been afraid of research.

He dove into his morning work, brain whirring in the background. Without the dead weight of school hanging over him, he had mental space for other things.

If his camera had caught evidence of vandalism that night, there'd be a court case. He opened a tab for the county courthouse and scanned the docket.

His breath stopped when he saw Alexei's name listed as the plaintiff in an upcoming case. The details were thin, but the charges were vandalism and destruction of property. Two weeks from now, Sasha's family might have all their problems solved, and the man who'd bothered them for months would be behind bars.

Sasha would be happy about that, but also probably mad she hadn't caught the guy herself. She was complex, like an onion. Lots of layers, and enough heat to make his eyes burn. But she'd been the one to teach him that onions took a long time to soften and turn sweet. Patience could be his friend in this situation.

He'd brainstorm the steps he could take, one at a time, to win her friendship back. Maybe seeing her face once in a while would be enough to satisfy the strange ache in his chest. He could go from seeing her to maybe saying hello. Once they were on speaking terms again, he could apologize for leaving her alone that night. Maybe even work toward becoming friends again one day.

What he absolutely did not let himself hope for was that they could ever be more than friends. The most he could wish for was to be back in her orbit, a moth to her flame.

Ben had said to follow the things that brought him joy, and this would have to be close enough.

Chapter 20

"It's too quiet." Dad dropped the blinds over the brand-new window of the food truck and turned to face Sasha. "I got used to always checking for them."

"I know what you mean," she said. "I keep looking around the corner, expecting something else to happen."

"I guess it might take some time to relax. But I'm glad it's over."

"Me too."

Everything was over, both the danger to the truck and the unlikely happiness she'd found with Cameron.

He hadn't contacted her in weeks, which was fair. She'd told him to go, and he'd gone.

God, but she'd been on her worst behavior that night.

At her last few therapy sessions, she couldn't stop herself from glancing upstairs as Matt walked her to the door. Cameron wasn't there, she'd told herself, but that didn't stop her from looking for him. As if he'd appear at any moment.

She'd been taking her therapy sessions a lot more seriously

since the night they'd broken up. Matt didn't think she had true anger management issues, and in that, he agreed with Cameron's assessment.

But her temper had caused her to make decisions she regretted, and Matt had given her even more techniques to slow her roll. He'd encouraged her to think about the roots of her anger, and why it was her first line of defense when she felt stressed.

"It's not a bad thing, fighting to keep yourself safe," he'd told her. "But I want you to think of a time you let down your guard with someone, and nothing bad happened."

She'd swallowed and hadn't come up with a good answer, because her mind had flooded her with memories of Cameron, who'd made her feel safe a hundred percent of the time. And she'd pushed him away because she hadn't trusted her gut on that feeling.

Matt was not only helping her sort out her anger issues. He'd also gotten her started on the process of clearing her record, now possible because of the new evidence they'd gathered. And because he'd helped her type out a full account of the six months of vandalism leading up to her fight. Something she hadn't bothered to explain to them before.

So all in all, lots of things in her life were looking up. She just couldn't seem to enjoy any of it.

She could have sworn she'd seen Cameron a few times lately, but it had to be her imagination, dreaming him up in places where he wasn't. She'd seen the back of a dark, curly head walking in the opposite direction as she'd left the square last night. Through the gym window the other day, she'd seen a car that looked like his. But then again, a lot of people had Cameron's car.

"So." Dad cleared his throat, interrupting her train of thought. "I have some news. About the truck. I wanted to wait until some of the excitement died down. But next week is our hearing, and the lawyer tells me he has every reason to believe we'll win."

"You'll be rich now," she teased.

After the criminal case ended with the vandal in jail, their civil case was moving ahead. Dad was pressing charges for the total damages done to the truck over the last six months, not just the one night.

"Not rich," he said. "But if we win, I'll have a lot more options than I've had in a long time."

He leaned against the counter, studying her. "I got an estimate on the total value of the truck while the insurance company was giving me the quote for the windows."

"You're trying to tell me you're selling the truck."

A month ago, she'd fought him on the idea. But now it didn't fill her with the same sense of dread. If Dad had extra money, he could make it work. Maybe look for a new job for a while, or even take a long break. Look at her, conquering her temper.

His brows went up. "You don't seem mad about it."

"I'm not. If it's what you want, I think you should do it."

"As it turns out…" He let the sentence hang for a moment. "I don't want to sell the truck. But I am alone a lot of the time, and as you've pointed out to me over and over, I'm getting older. So I must need extra help."

"We all need help. It's not about your age."

He crossed his massive arms over his chest. "I'm not sure I believed you about that before. But I do see the benefits now. And sometimes, I do wish for…company. A partner. So Anya and I decided we're going to combine our businesses. We're looking into buying a bigger truck. If we both sell, we could make it work."

She stood up straighter. "That's an amazing idea."

A smile turned up the corner of his mouth. "You don't say that to me very often. It must really be a good idea."

"You'll have help when you need it, and you help her out so much, too. You'll be able to pool staffing, maybe take more days off."

Dad held up a hand, palm up. "I didn't say anything about more days off."

She rolled her eyes. "Fine. No extra days off. But more help."

She paused, another thought occurring to her.

"You didn't want me to take over the business? I mean, you've always said—"

"No. I want you to have your own life. This isn't what you worked for. Other things are meant for you. Bigger things."

"I'm not sure teaching martial arts counts as bigger things."

His expression turned serious. "You will do even more than that. I know you. You fight to the top. And you'll have more in your life because of it. Not just a better job, but more happiness. More of what you love."

She swallowed. "I haven't been doing so well in that department so far."

He shook his head. "I don't know about that. You have me. And Anya and Kiran. And Cameron."

"You know I haven't seen him in weeks."

"Doesn't matter. That boy is in love with you."

She froze, her hand on the counter. "Why would you—How do you know that?"

"I recognized it the first time I met him. Plain as day on his face."

She pushed away from the counter, crossing the space and busying herself unloading the dishwasher.

"I think you're wrong."

"I'm never wrong. Just like you are also never wrong. The only part I can't tell yet is if you love him back."

She dropped the baking tray into the sink, the loud crash echoing in the closed space. Retrieving it, she dried it a second time with a dish towel.

"We don't need to have this conversation, because I'm not going to see him again."

Of course she didn't love Cameron. She missed him. She'd felt attached to him, and safe around him, but that wasn't the same thing as love.

There'd been one moment, when they'd been out to dinner, when she'd thought he was about to say something. He'd had feelings, but she'd stopped him from telling her. And by now, he'd definitely changed his mind.

She hadn't heard from him, and she didn't deserve to, after the way they'd left things that night.

Dad approached her from the side and put a hand on her shoulder. "I'll leave you be. No sense poking the bear. But just because you haven't seen him doesn't mean he doesn't still love you. Love doesn't disappear so fast. If you do see him again, you can ask him for yourself."

"Ask him, huh." She scrubbed at a new tray. "It worked out really well when I asked Anya if you guys were dating."

"Ha." A laugh burst out of him. "I'm sure she put you right. Anya would rather poke out her eye than ever marry again. It's not her nature."

"I know that. Now."

"Did you also know," he said, his eyes twinkling, "that a

momo is not very different from a knish? We've been talking about trying a curry knish."

"A new recipe? That's huge."

He nodded, his expression turning serious. "I haven't let myself try a new recipe in twenty years. Not since… But you know, it's probably time."

"That sounds good. I'd eat a curry knish. And I think they're called samosas."

He clapped her on the back. "Then you'll get one of the first batches."

He left her to finish the dishes and stomped out to the car to go to the grocery store.

* * *

Six days later, they met in the courthouse for the civil trial. The polished wood of the foyer squeaked under her sneakers as she and Dad made their way to the waiting area. Dad looked nervous. He'd never liked bureaucratic offices, and she must have inherited that trait from him. This building, however clean and official-looking it was, gave her the creeps.

It was too quiet, too full of its own importance. Lawyers strode past in their crisp, dark suits, so certain of their place here, so sure they were on the side of right, the side of the rules. Those types of men had never done one good thing for her.

When their lawyer approached them, they both stood immediately, and he led them into the soundproofed courtroom. She shivered, memories of her probation hearing making her stomach churn. For once, she'd skipped breakfast.

They sat through a series of short cases. Their turn came next, and she turned to look at Dad. His profile was grim, staring straight ahead as the judge read the charges.

This moment meant more to Dad than he'd let on. The truck had been his family's only support, the dream he and his wife had built together. It meant something—that he could be paid back now for his loss. For both of their losses.

Twenty minutes later, the gavel banged down. They'd been awarded the highest amount of damages possible.

Dad turned and pulled her into a tight hug.

"You did it," she told him.

"We did it together."

For once in her life, justice had been done. And it wasn't just their efforts that had brought it about. Cameron had believed this was possible from the start, and he'd helped her at every step.

Her throat tightened on a sudden rush of missing him. She hadn't seen his face in over a month. She missed his warm, hazel eyes and practical brain. She missed his steadiness and how he understood her.

As they stood from their seats and filed out, she realized she didn't have anything to be mad at anymore. The unfairness had been punished.

If she stayed mad, then the only person she had to be mad at was herself, beating against the walls of her own limitations. And she didn't want to live like that.

Cameron had understood that about her. He'd reminded her she wasn't an angry person, just a person with anger.

She missed him so fiercely that as they stepped out of the courthouse onto the manicured lawn, she imagined she saw him, his lean, dark form walking away from the building, out into the parking lot.

But that *was* him. She recognized the lanky stride, the flash of sunlight off his wire-rimmed glasses.

Her legs took off running across the asphalt without her permission.

She called his name as he reached his car, and he whipped around to face her, his expression nervous.

"What are you doing here?" The breath puffed out of her after her short run, and she fought to keep her tone level.

The sight of him had exploded a ball of feelings inside her chest, sweet and light. She fought the urge to throw herself at him.

He tilted his head to the side, the movement familiar and awkward. "I, uh. I *was* going to try to talk to you at some point. But I thought it was too soon? Anyway, I wanted to be there today. As moral support. Congratulations on the win."

"You've been checking up on me." He had been there, those other nights. She hadn't imagined it.

His face flushed a dull red. "I'm not trying to be creepy. I thought I could start small. You know, little steps."

"Little steps to what?"

"To talking to you again. And maybe being your friend, if you want that. Sasha, I'm sorry. I realized I wasn't a very good friend to you that night. You told me that's all you wanted from me, and I left you there alone."

Her throat tightened. "You're apologizing. To me."

"I need to. For there to be any chance…"

"You want us to be friends."

His expression turned almost wistful. "If that's a possibility, then yes."

Chapter 20

She did throw herself at him then. The breath rushed out of him as she pulled him into a tight hug. His arms went around her a second later, and she felt his chest rise and fall against hers. His hands shook on her back, and a moment later, she felt his cheek land on the top of her head.

"I missed you," she told him.

She hugged him tighter to her chest, recognition blooming inside her. This feeling was love. It had been a long time since she'd felt it for anyone new, anyone who wasn't family.

But he was the only one she wanted to be with. The only one she felt safe with, felt like herself with.

He was the one.

"I missed you, too," he said.

"I need to apologize to you, too. I'm sorry for how I acted that night. I was over the line, and I knew it. I'm so bad at waiting."

"I know you are." She could hear the smile in his voice.

She tilted her head back to look up at him. "But I'm working on my anger issues. For real, now. I know I'll be better from here on out."

"I like your anger. Because it's part of who you are."

His eyes darkened, roaming over her face. She recognized that look, too. But he wasn't asking for more. Yet.

Maybe they could find their way into a relationship over time, though she'd never been all that patient once she'd decided on something.

"Yes. We can be friends again," she told him.

He gave a serious nod.

She drew in a breath and took a step back from him. "And that's all you want? To be just friends?"

"I—" Cameron looked as if his brain had glitched, and she

hung on his moment of hesitation.

He pulled himself together enough to reply. "I don't want to ask you for too much right now. Or for anything you don't want to give."

The bubble of lightness in her chest expanded until it was a wonder she didn't float away across the parking lot.

That wasn't a no. He wanted her. And she wanted him right back. How to make that happen was the next problem to tackle.

"I think we should get together sometime. Tomorrow, maybe." No time like the present.

"Tomorrow," he echoed, looking shocked.

"Yep. And we'll see what we think after that."

Chapter 21

Cameron knocked on Sasha's apartment door at 7:00 p.m. the next night, unsure of what to expect. It wasn't a date. She'd said, "We'll see what we think."

He'd overanalyzed that sentence the last twenty-four hours in a way only he could. She'd asked him if friends was all he wanted them to be.

A dozen times since yesterday, he'd cursed himself for not saying what he wanted. How was she supposed to know how he felt if he never told her?

But slow and steady had to be the right way in this situation. Work carefully toward the goal, and it had a better chance of happening. She deserved a strong foundation, with careful planning.

He froze as she opened the door, all careful planning leaving his brain. She was not wearing her usual jeans and a tank top.

Instead, she wore a skintight silver minidress that hugged her astonishing curves, plus her usual black leather jacket. She'd slicked her hair back from her face and painted her mouth bright red, and her brow piercing glinted in the hallway light.

This was too much. He couldn't be expected to carry on a normal conversation with her looking like this. She looked like a fantasy from one of his comic books, come to life.

He cleared his throat. "You look, uh. You look good. I think I'm underdressed."

"You're not underdressed. Come on in."

He followed her into her apartment, where he'd never been invited before. She'd always come to him, or else they'd been at the truck.

Her space was an expression of her personality, with sleek wood floors, black furniture, and bold abstract art pieces on the walls. The splashes of color were like her, as was the clutter on the coffee table and chairs. A mix of bright and messy, and all of it looking much more lived-in than his place.

"Do you want to sit?" she asked. "I thought maybe we should talk for a bit before we go out?"

She gestured to the dark leather couch, and he sat. The only problem with this arrangement was that now there was nowhere else to look but at her. His eyes devoured her. He couldn't stop them this time. He hadn't seen her in so long, his brain was on the verge of overload.

It didn't help that as she sat, he could now see most of her leg, and the dragon tattoo inked up the side of her thigh. He jerked his eyes upward to find her studying him, and felt the flush crawl up his neck.

She didn't look like she felt even a hint of nerves. She looked happy, relaxed. Excited to see him, which seemed highly improbable.

"First of all, I want to thank you," she said. "For lending us the camera. What you did helped Dad so much. Helped all of us."

"It was nothing. I'm glad it worked out in the end."

"I had a long time to think about it, and I realized something else. You helped me, but you didn't do it for me. You gave me what I needed to solve the problem on my own."

"You didn't need me to do anything for you. You just needed the right tools."

"And that's what no one's gotten about me before," she went on. "They'd either tell me I was doing things wrong and fight me about it, or try to take charge and make decisions for me. And neither of those worked. I guess what I'm trying to say is, you *were* a good friend to me. Don't think you weren't."

He swallowed. "I'm glad if I helped. But I want to do better."

She leaned forward, putting a hand on his knee and further scrambling his thoughts. "What you did for me… That's what partners do. People who are on the same team. You didn't let me hurt myself, and you found other ways to help me."

His pulse thundered in his ears. "You helped me, too. You made me eat and sleep."

She laughed, the sound rich and happy. "I was good at that much, at least."

"More than that. You were good at more than that."

He hadn't planned to say this much tonight, but she was here, and close, and happy, and she was wearing that dress. Incautious words tumbled out of his mouth.

"You made me feel things again. I was… I know it sounds cheesy, but I was kind of dead inside when you met me. Burnt out. I wanted to quit my job, quit school. But then I had a taste of happiness. Of what life could be like when you…when you care about someone. And that changed everything for me. I know what I need now. I postponed my graduation and my study. I'm giving myself more time and I'm taking care of myself. And the reason why is that I have someone I want to be there for."

Her eyes had widened during his speech, and she'd leaned forward until her chest almost touched his arm. He could feel her warmth through his sleeve.

"Am I...the someone?" she asked, her heart in her eyes.

He brought his hand up to the side of her face. "Of course you're the someone. Sasha, I love you. I know that might not change anything for you. But I can't stop myself."

"Well, that is very convenient." She swiped under each eye with a finger. "Because I love you, too."

He froze, because it was too much, too soon, and yet it was happening anyway. In a rush, his life flipped around, realigned itself, and his future fell into place in front of him.

"Cameron? You look like your circuits overloaded."

"I'm just...really happy right now."

"Does that mean I can kiss you?"

"Yes. You should absolutely do that."

Then she was in his arms, climbing into his lap and laying her mouth on his, and he was probably getting red lipstick over most of his face, but it didn't matter. Her weight against him was perfect, the feel of her hair under his fingers, and her soft curves against his chest. All of it, a hundred percent perfect.

She pulled away from the kiss a minute later, her chest rising and falling.

"You didn't want to go to dinner right now, did you?"

"We can skip one meal."

She grinned down at him. "I wore this dress to seduce you after dinner. But it worked faster than I thought."

"Things always move fast with you. But I like it."

"Good." She nipped his jaw, kissed her way down his neck. "Because I can't wait."

* * *

Later, she did feed him dinner. She'd pulled on his shirt— a sight he'd never get tired of—and gone to the kitchen, instructing him to stay put. The garment was six inches too long, but fit her too tight across the chest.

Propped up in her big bed, with soft black sheets pooled around his waist, he waited for her return. He wasn't used to being waited on, and the urge to get up and check on her was strong.

He wanted to finish their earlier conversation. Telling someone you loved them was a huge step, but his brain already wanted to know what that meant, and what came next. He wanted the next weeks and months with her, but he hadn't planned far enough in advance to know what to say in this situation.

How did you ask the woman you loved for a long-term commitment? Because that's what he wanted. And it seemed like with Sasha, directness was the best policy.

She returned carrying a box of crackers, a plate of sliced cheese and strawberries, and two water bottles under her arm. She pitched one of the bottles at him, and he caught it.

"Hydration," she told him. "And snacks. I have to go get a couple more things."

She disappeared down the hallway again, and he took a long

swig of water, wondering what came next. He'd never lack for surprises with Sasha as his girlfriend.

He rolled the word around in his mind. Girlfriend was somehow not right, not enough for what she meant to him.

When she came back again, she had a paper shopping bag looped over her arm and a bouquet of purple flowers in her hand.

"I got you these, but I was too distracted earlier to give them to you." She held out the bouquet to him, and he took it automatically.

"You got me flowers."

She slid one hip onto the edge of the bed next to him. "I felt bad about leaving the flowers you got me in your car that night. So I wanted to replace them. Women can give men flowers, you know."

She fixed him with a look that said arguing otherwise would be pointless.

"Of course they can," he agreed. "I just feel bad I didn't bring you anything. I was trying to take things slow."

The corner of her mouth turned up. "Well, I wasn't. I got you a couple more things, too."

"But you don't owe me anything."

"I guess I wanted to show you that you're important to me. When I saw you yesterday, after not seeing you for so long, I felt... I don't know how to say it. Like I was going to explode if I didn't hug you. Like I *needed* to. That makes no sense."

"It makes perfect sense." He reached for her hand, threading their fingers together. "Sasha, I know we said we loved each other. But I want to make sure both of us know what that means. I want... I wish we could be together long-term. In whatever way we decide. We can take it slow and see how you feel. But you're my person."

"And you're my person too." Her hand squeezed his. "For as long as you want me."

"That's going to be a long time."

"Good." She gave a decisive nod. "So we're trying this whole relationship thing. I've never done it, but it can't be that hard."

A laugh burst out of him. "Again, this is all happening faster than I expected. But I should change my expectations."

"Expectations are overrated," she said. "And now that's settled, you get your other presents. First, this."

She reached into the bag and pulled out a plastic-wrapped copy of a comic. He froze when he saw the cover.

"Where did you find this?" He'd only been searching for this issue for a decade.

"Where do you think?" she asked with a grin. "Luka told me he had it in stock the last time we were there, and he knew you wanted it. But he wanted to make sure you were 'good for me' before he let you have it. I promised him you were very good for me."

"I don't know what to say. I don't deserve this."

"I think you do. You deserve to have fun. And speaking of fun…"

She pulled out a cardboard box, the last item in her shopping bag, and set it on his lap.

"Open it," she told him.

"Why do I not trust that gleam in your eye?"

"You'll like it, I promise. I'll make sure you do."

He flipped open the cardboard lid to reveal a small assortment of sex toys. He stared at them, mind already racing ahead to all their possible uses. He'd need to test each of them out thoroughly.

"You're blushing," she told him.

"I think I'm done talking now," he said, and dove for her.

Chapter 22

Ten months later

Cameron stood, hands on his hips, looking out the large bay window of his brand-new, empty office. Flurries of snow dusted the bare branches of the trees, glowing white in the streetlights. It got dark early these days, but the days were growing longer, stretching into spring.

Tonight, he'd stayed late at Ben's request.

Sasha's arms slid around his waist, hugging him from behind. The warm press of her body against his back filled him with a rush of contentment.

"Happy birthday," she said, pressing her face between his shoulder blades.

He turned in her arms and pressed a kiss to her mouth.

"It's been a good birthday so far."

"Much better than last year," she agreed. "And when we get home, it'll be even better."

He groaned. "Don't tease me right now. My boss is about to walk through the door."

Her eyes twinkled up at him. "I'll stop. For now."

"It's also the one-year anniversary of the day we met," he told her.

"I remember it well. I walked in and found this very attractive man, dressed like someone from the wrong century, asleep at my counselor's desk." She snapped his suspender with a finger.

"So it was the suspenders that drew you in, is what you're saying."

"Definitely." Her expression sobered. "I'm glad you fell asleep at that desk, though."

"Not as glad as I am."

Looking down at her, he was lost for further words, lost in her brown and blue eyes that held the whole world.

A loud throat-clearing from the doorway brought both their heads around.

"Don't let us interrupt anything," Vanessa announced loudly as she walked in. "We know you're in the honeymoon phase of the relationship, and anything could happen in the next five minutes."

"Ignore her," Ben said, following her in the door. "She acts like she knows a thing or two about relationships."

Vanessa elbowed him in the side and turned a dazzling smile on them. "I love a new couple, what can I say? And I'm so proud of you, Cameron."

An unfamiliar pressure swelled behind his breastbone. These people were as dear to him as family. Vanessa had gotten him the admin assistant job in the first place, and Ben had been his idol for as long as he could remember.

That he was a full-time therapist on staff now hadn't quite sunk in.

Sasha slid out of his arms, but gripped his hand in her own. On her arm, the ink from her new tattoo flashed—an Aquarius constellation, wrapped around her wrist like a bracelet.

"He's been talking about nothing else but setting up his new practice," she said. "I told him I'd help decorate the space. But if he lets me do it, it'll have a lot of colors."

"Colors are good for him." Vanessa nodded approvingly. "Don't let him get too stuffy and boring in his old age."

"Hey," Cameron interjected. "Thirty is the new twenty."

Ben and Vanessa exchanged glances.

"Babies," Vanessa muttered.

"That's what I was thinking," Ben said.

He held up the bottle of champagne in his hand. "Anyway, if you were wondering why I asked you to stay late, this is why. We need to have a celebratory toast before you launch your practice next month."

"I brought the glasses." Vanessa held up her hands, champagne flutes threaded between her fingers.

Ben popped the cork and poured the champagne. Vanessa handed each of them a glass.

Cameron cleared his throat, clutching the stem of the crystal. "I want to say thank you to you both. To all of you. This last year has been… A lot of it wasn't easy. But if I'd known this was the reward for all the hard work, I'd do it all again."

"You deserve it, and much more," Ben said.

"Hear, hear," Vanessa added.

"And I want to toast Sasha, for helping me have fun again."

He smiled down at the woman he loved, and her answering expression lit him up inside.

"You haven't seen anything yet," she said, and held up her glass. "To hard work, and to having fun."

"I'll drink to that," Vanessa said.

"And to The Well Space," Ben said, holding his glass high. "To what we've created, and what we'll do next."

They drained their glasses, and Ben clapped Cameron on the back. "Welcome aboard, my friend."

"Thank you," he said. "This means the world to me."

After they'd gone, he pulled Sasha back into his arms, tucking her head under his chin. They stood for a long time by the window, watching the snow.

"And thank you," he told her. "Thank you for being here with me."

"Always," she answered.

He thanked himself for taking a chance. Thanked the world for bringing her to him.

Thank you for my life, he thought, and pressed a kiss to the top of her head. *Thank you for the life we'll have together.*

Afterword

Thank you so much for reading this book! If you enjoyed it, please consider leaving a review on your platform of choice. Reviews help boost indie authors so much. And if you'd like to keep in touch, you can join my newsletter, and you'll receive updates about all my new releases, book sales, and bonus stories.

As usual, I have so many people to thank, all of whom helped this book come into existence. To my beta readers, Brianna and Alona, thank you for all your insight and feedback about what was working and not working in the book. To my editor, Charlie Knight, thank you for pointing out so many things which made this manuscript immeasurably stronger. I know I love an emotional support comma...

Thank you to my family. Your unending support lifts me up, always. And thank you to my cats, for sitting in front of the computer monitor when I needed to see it, and for always keeping me company. That's true love.

To my online writing groups, particularly the Baguettes, thank you for your support, understanding, and all of my daily laughs.

Lastly, to you. Thank you for reading this book.

About the Author

S.M. Levine grew up with her face in a book, and now she writes steamy, emotional contemporary romance about imperfect people who find true love. She lives in the Midwest with her family and a small assortment of cats.

You can connect with me on:

🌐 https://www.smlevineauthor.com

🖇 https://www.instagram.com/sm_levine

Subscribe to my newsletter:

✉ https://www.smlevineauthor.com

Also by S.M. Levine

Check out these other titles in The Well Space series!

The Well Space Series:

Less than Perfect

Trial Run

Couples Session

Over Work